HOUSE 23

HOUSE 23

A Thriller

ELI YANCE

Skyhorse Publishing

Skyhorse Publishing books may be purchased in bulk at special discounts for sales promotion, corporate gifts, fund-raising, or educational purposes. Special editions can also be created to specifications. For details, contact the Special Sales Department, Skyhorse Publishing, 307 West 36th Street, 11th Floor, New York, NY 10018 or info@skyhorsepublishing.com.

Skyhorse® and Skyhorse Publishing® are registered trademarks of Skyhorse Publishing, Inc.®, a Delaware corporation.

Visit our website at www.skyhorsepublishing.com.

10 9 8 7 6 5 4 3 2 1

Library of Congress Cataloging-in-Publication Data is available on file.

Cover design by Lilith_C (lilithcgraphics)
Cover photo credit: Fotolia

Print ISBN: 978-1-940456-74-4
Ebook ISBN: 978-1-940456-75-1

Printed in the United States of America

To my mother, for everything

1

February 2014

"How do you feel in general?"

"Empty."

"Empty?"

"Empty, hollow, vacant, blank, bare. Empty, I feel empty. You don't understand?"

"I understand. I just want more details."

"I don't like your tone. It's incredibly general, professional—dull and boring, if you like, but I'm not here to judge, I guess that's *your* job." A pause, an evaluation, a summary. "Devoid of accent, clean, standard. Did you go to a public school?"

"I don't think it's relevant."

"Not relevant?" Joseph Lee reclined back into the poor comfort of his chair. His back rested against the thin padding, woven into a tartan design and worn well with age. He sighed and stared at the woman in front of him, sitting in a much more comfortable leather seat, her legs crossed and her glasses hanging on the bridge of her nose. Her eyes were fierce yet soft, professional yet powerful; they met Joseph's stare over the desk.

"What if I said it would make me more comfortable to know? Would that make it relevant?"

She unfolded her legs and rolled her chair closer to the desk. She rested a notepad on her lap and waved a pen over it. "Yes, I *did* go to a public school," she admitted, her eyes still pouring their ferocity into the face of the man opposite.

Joseph grinned and leaned forward. "So, Doctor Marsh," he said slowly, sitting back again, somewhat agitated and uncomfortable. "Do you think I'm insane?"

"What happened was . . . " The doctor paused and sucked the tip of her pen anxiously. Her eyes switched from Joseph to her notepad, which showed very little.

"Awful?" Joseph offered. "Horrific? Terrible? Pick one and say it. I'm not a walking thesaurus, you know."

"Unquestionable," she said, regaining her composure.

"They *asked* me questions about it."

"That's not what I meant."

"I know," he paused, his eyes boring into those of the psychiatrist. "This is not a foregone conclusion you know, far from it in fact. I didn't do it."

"I never said anything to the contrary, Mr. Lee."

"But you *thought* it."

Doctor Marsh shifted in her chair, the plush leather squeaked underneath her backside. "Lets, just for a moment, imagine you *did* do it," she said. "Do you understand what could—*could have*—happened to you? Do you understand the seriousness of the situation?"

Joseph propelled himself forward in his chair again. "Life in jail," he pondered brashly. "Could it get more serious? What about Death Row, would you consider that a harsher sentence?"

"This is England, Mr. Lee," she pointed out. "There *is* no Death Row, there is *no* death sentence."

"Yet there *is* a life sentence," Lee said with a smile. "A life sentence and a death sentence." He repeated the words numerous times. "You see, a life sentence sounds . . . minimal. It's life, after all—we all live and life *is* just a sentence; it has a beginning, middle, and an end, the full stop being your final breath. A death sentence on the other hand sounds rather bleak. In fact, it sounds fucking ominous, and death has no beginning or middle, just an end.

"It's like prison, really . . . only without the beginning and the middle. You die and you die alone. You get wrapped in a body bag and buried six feet under with a two-foot, shitty fucking tombstone provided by the council. People piss on graves, you know—people destroy them and deface them, kids mostly; it's a game to them. It's the circle of life. First you're born, you get a few years of bliss, and then you get pissed and shit on until you die. When you're stiff and ready, they stick you six feet underground, you get a few years of peace and silence, and then you get pissed on again."

"Are you going anywhere with this, Mr. Lee?"

"No, but I like to talk, you're a shrink. You're paid to listen."

"Tell me something else then, Mr. Lee," she said, her eyes fixed on the dark orbs of her patient. "What happened last Christmas?"

December 2013

Joseph Lee watched the digital clock nudge onto 6:32 and sighed. All day he'd lounged inside the confines of his living room. Christmas depressed him. It was for children and religion; adults had no place in the glittering holiday. No longer were gifts given and accepted with warmth and love; the love had died. Christmas was a time for running up credit card bills and bingeing on chocolate and alcohol.

More people committed suicide at Christmastime than at any other time of year. More people decided to climb behind the wheels of their cars drunk than at any other time of year.

For the people who have friends and family, Christmas is an expensive, overindulgent holiday; for the people without, it's a depressing reminder of a life they don't have.

He opened another can of beer and drank half, burping loudly after the liquid settled on his stomach.

"Aren't you going to get ready?"

He turned toward the figure in the doorway: a tall, beautiful young woman—her hands on her hips, a stern look on her face.

He mumbled something even he couldn't understand.

"Well?" she strode into the room. He watched her and smiled—the swaying of her slim hips, the slight swing of her firm backside clad tightly in dark denim, the subtle movement of her large breasts beneath a thin white blouse.

She took a seat opposite him.

He stared at her for a while. She had amazing blue eyes, thin lips covered with dark red lipstick, and supple skin. Her blouse was cut into a V shape, exposing her cleavage. His eyes followed a silver necklace that hung down her neckline. On the end of the chain, a sapphire set in white gold dangled just above her voluptuous breasts.

"Stop staring at my tits, Joseph," she said lightly. "Answer me, would you?"

"Why do I have to get dressed?"

"It's half past six, it's dark outside, and you still haven't changed out of your dressing gown."

"It's Christmas, Jennifer," he explained. "I'm allowed to be lazy."

"We have guests coming in a couple of hours."

"Do we?"

"Sandra and Alan. Your brother, for God's sake. You arranged it. They'll be here at eight, remember?"

Joseph shrugged and took another sip from his can. "Now that you mention it, yes, I remember."

"Well, are you going to get dressed?"

He paused and studied his wife again. She was as perfect as she had been three years ago when he had taken her hand in marriage.

"Fine," he relented. "I'll go and throw some clothes on." He rose from the chair and drained the rest of his drink, putting the empty can on the floor. "Just let me get a shower and a shave first."

"Okay," Jennifer agreed, frowning at the empty can on the floor. "Brush your teeth, as well. Freshen up a bit. You stink of booze."

———

Joseph tossed his gown carelessly on the floor in the master bedroom. The creased heap of sweat-clogged cotton collapsed in a bundle near the bed. Standing naked in front of a wall-length mirror, he admired his body.

He wasn't a well-built man, but he wasn't skinny or fat either. He worked out in his younger days and jogged every other morning.

He sucked in his bloated stomach and sighed the air back out.

After a few months of marriage, his fitness plans had completely spiraled out of control. Instead of a high-protein breakfast, pasta lunches, and snacks from cereal bars, protein shakes, and isotonic drinks, he opted for fast food, chocolate, and beer. He had a beautiful woman who had sworn to love him regardless, but he had abused that privilege.

Despite the years of neglect, his metabolism had managed to keep his body in decent shape. His belly was protruding and the rest of him was built with extra layers of fat, but underneath it all was plenty of muscle waiting to be unleashed. He was sure one day he would get back into the running and the weight training, but he wasn't quite sure when that day would be.

After checking every angle of his naked flesh in the mirror, he walked to the ensuite. His bare feet rubbed against the soft bedroom carpet and left tracks—footprints in fluffy snow. He opened the shower door, turned on the shower, and watched his face in the bathroom mirror as the water heated up.

He was still good looking, or so he told himself, but the toil of the last few days—the lazy, indulgent nature of the holidays—was showing. Stubble popped through his skin and blackened his face, his lips were dry and flaky, and his eyes were heavy, almost black. Before the hot water steamed up the mirror and covered his features, he splashed two handfuls of cold water over his face. It did little to aid his appearance but it woke him up a little.

As the steam flowed, turning the small ensuite into a sauna, he reached for a portable music player on the counter, swamped by a collection of soaps and shower gels. He flicked through the channels on the MP3 player until he found the one he sought, then, with a jiggle of his naked behind, he mimed the words to Metallica's "Master of Puppets" as the notes filtered through the dense, steamy air.

He turned the music up all the way, stepped through the wall of steam, and disappeared into his own world.

February 2014

Doctor Claire Marsh leaned back in her chair, waiting for more. Joseph Lee stopped talking.

"And?" she pushed.

"There is no *and*," Joseph said placidly. "That's all I can remember."

"The last thing you remember is standing in the shower?"

"Yes."

"What about your wife?"

"I don't know what she was doing. I was in the shower, remember?"

The doctor tapped the tip of her pen against her front teeth, her eyes focused on the floor. "Did you often argue with your wife?"

"Arguing gets you nowhere," Joseph said lightly. The doctor lifted her eyes and stared at him. "I preferred to kick the shit out of her."

She paused, looked for a twinkle in Lee's eyes, and then continued. "Can you please be serious about this?"

"But that's what you want to hear, isn't it?"

"Not necessarily. I think you're misreading my intentions."

"Bullshit," Joseph snapped. "You're digging for violence, domestic disturbance. You'd be delighted if I was a drunken, wife-beating lowlife; it would make your job so much easier, wouldn't it?"

She remained silent, staring at Lee.

"I'm not a violent person," Lee said, calming down.

She nodded. "I said nothing to the contrary."

"But you think I did it. I'm a human being in mourning. You want to turn me into a statistic."

"I just want to know what happened, I want the truth."

"You don't give a shit about the truth. You care about your own job, your own life. That's the way the world works. You just want the easy way out, the easy answers. You want my guilt. My guilt puts your face on the front page."

Doctor Marsh disregarded the comment. "What was the next thing you remember after climbing into the shower?"

December 2013

He woke with a start; his eyes sprung open. His lungs burst into an instantaneous applause on awakening, coughing fluid.

Jets of hot water purged from the shower head, raining onto the slumped figure curled underneath. While near-scalding water hit his face, Joseph Lee felt the urge to move.

His legs propped open the shower door. While the top half of his body had been relaxing inside the shower, his bottom half had slumped outside.

"What the fuck . . ." he mumbled, trickles of water spilling from his mouth. He lifted his head but soon wished he hadn't.

A shooting pain, starting at the base of his skull, raced around his brain, sticking needles in every crevice before leaving a painful throb in its wake.

He moved his hand toward the pain, brushing the back of his head with his palm and inspecting the result. A smear of crimson stuck to his hand before the jets washed it away. He brushed his hand against his head again, as though he needed confirmation. Again his palm was smeared with blood—not a large amount but enough to cause him concern.

He mumbled distasteful and incoherent slurs as he watched blue stars dance in the corner of his eyes. He tried to push his body up but the shower's wet plastic surface rejected his grip and he fell face-first into a pool of water that had accumulated around the plughole. He felt his front tooth crack. A chunk of enamel broke free and pushed through his upper lip, spraying blood across his face.

He clawed at the walls, managed to propel himself to his knees. He rested back on his heels and tilted his head upward, inviting the hot jets of water to wash away the blood and soothe the pain. Spots of blood had sprayed up his nose. The thick fluid had stuck to nostrils hairs, leaving a sickly coppery stench.

He took in gulps of water, swishing them around in his mouth and spitting out the diluted crimson concoction until the taste and smell of his own blood had been reduced to a minor annoyance.

He looked up and, with a dreary expression, shouted as loud as he could: "Hello!" he sprayed pink globs onto the half-open shower screen. "Jennifer!" Every screamed syllable cut through his nerves like a cold knife.

He reached forward, hoping to grasp the shower door. His hand fell short and he collapsed, tumbling out of the shower and onto the dripping floor. The music was still blaring. Crunching guitars, thudding drums, and heavy bass pounded his weary head. He left the noise behind and slowly dragged himself, on his hands and knees, out of the bathroom and across the bedroom.

On the carpeted hallway, several feet from the staircase, he lifted his head and screamed again, calling for his wife, calling for help. The throbbing pulse in his ear drums canceled out any chance of a coherent reply. Blood dripped down his chin; he could feel the thick fluid fusing with his saliva and forming on his tongue and gums. The taste of copper was prominent enough to make him gag.

He crawled to the banister at the top of the stairs and used the wooden stand to climb to his feet. Immediately he struggled to keep his balance, his legs turned to jelly, the strength sucked out of his body. Adrenaline forced him to continue. He slowly made his way down the stairs, careful with every step he took.

Every footfall sent a bolt of pain through his body. From the tips of his toes to the top of his head, agony poured through him.

He gripped the banister tightly with both hands as he made his way, smearing red carnage on the oak. His blurred eyes wobbled around his skull, causing the room to spin and vibrate. His vision allowed his eyes to scan only a small area, so he focused them on his wobbly feet, careful not to lose his footing.

When he reached the bottom of the staircase, he made a painful misjudgment and missed the bottom step. He toppled over like a rag doll, his knees smacked the edge of the uncarpeted stair, twisting and crunching under the impact. He screamed in anguish, falling chest-first onto the wooden corridor at the bottom of the staircase.

He rolled over several times, tossing and turning. He stopped when his body came into contact with something solid. Something moist and warm. Breathing heavily, blood freely pouring from his head and mouth, tears streaming from his eyes, he cursed several times, spitting every bloody syllable as if the words were poison.

He reached around in the darkness of his hazy eyes, hoping to find something that would supply enough leverage to pull him to his feet. His hand rested on the object that had stopped his incessant and excruciating rolling.

He paused, examining the object with a careful and wary touch. He rolled his hand over warm fabric, traced his fingers across soaked cotton. The tip of his forefinger found its way into a soft, oozing opening.

His heart skipped several beats as a disturbing realization dawned on him. Rolling away, he pushed himself up with the aid of his elbows and stared at the mangled body of his wife.

Jennifer Lee looked back at him through empty and cloudy eyes, her clothes soaked in her own blood. Across her abdomen, where Joseph's fingers had traced, her top had been ripped to expose her soft skin and several deep cuts. She lay in a pool of her own blood, the red fluid still dripping from numerous wounds and dribbling out of her open mouth.

February 2014

Joseph Lee stared deeply into the eyes of the female psychiatrist. A look of sympathy hid behind her professional gaze, but her curiosity and professional manner froze it out.

"I see her face every time I sleep," he said softly, his head held low.

The doctor nodded slowly, her eyes fixed on his averted gaze. "When was the last time you slept?"

"Properly? A week, maybe two."

"I understand."

Lee raised his head. "Do you? *How* could you? I lost my wife, I saw her mutilated body, I *touched* her wounds." He cringed at the memory. "I loved her. No one should have to go through what I went through. And, to top it off, the police made me the prime fucking suspect. Everyone thinks I killed her; even my own family have turned their backs on me."

"The police were just doing their job."

"And what a great job they did. Two months on and they still don't know who killed her or why. They're far too preoccupied with trying to drag a confession out of me. That's why you're here, after all—you're the last resort. The law couldn't do jack-shit, the lie detector proved inconclusive, the evidence was minimal to say the least. If they wasted less time on me and spent more time doing actual police work, then the bastard who killed Jennifer could be locked up by now!"

"I am here for your health, Mr. Lee," she assured. "This is an assessment of your mental status. You *do* have a history of mental illness—"

He was quick to interject. "That doesn't mean I'm capable of murder."

The psychiatrist leaned forward in her chair. "Look," she began, her voice full of reason. "In all fairness to the police, you had a motive. The house was in your wife's name, you have no personal fortune, and you haven't worked in years—"

Lee opened his mouth to object, but Doctor Marsh quickly continued before he could interrupt. "I *know* that's no basis for murder and I'm not implying anything of the sort, but you did stand to gain a lot of money, as well as a house, cars, bank accounts, and a significantly large life insurance policy. The police found no evidence at the scene, no witnesses, no sign of a break-in, and your fingerprints were the only ones found on the body—"

"So you're suggesting I killed my wife and then beat the shit out of myself?"

"I'm not suggesting anything. I'm not here to take sides."

Lee nodded. "Fair enough. So, after two months of harassment, you have the final say. The police have finished with me. I don't think they believe I didn't kill my wife, but they have no choice: they can't arrest me, they can't touch me. They didn't get a confession and you certainly won't." He leaned back in his chair, offering the doctor an unblinking stare. "Which means you're here to assess me, so *assess* me. Do I need help? Counseling? Maybe some brain-numbing medications? Or do you simply want to throw me in the nut house?"

Doctor Marsh smiled and shook her head. "You have issues, Mr. Lee," she surmised. "Which isn't surprising after what happened, but you need to understand that the world isn't out to get you. If you want help, I can give you help. I strongly recommend that you take my offer of counseling, some regular sessions perhaps. Having a professional to talk to can help you get through this." She paused, almost expecting Lee to interrupt. He remained silent. "We could also look at sleeping tablets and possibly some anti-depressants or something to calm your mood. It's up to you. No one is forcing you into anything."

Lee smiled and stood. "In that case, I'll be saying good-bye. I don't want any pills and I certainly don't want anyone to talk to. I prefer to block out the memories; talking about them just keeps them alive."

2

Six months later

J oseph Lee woke with a start. His eyes jerked open—a raspy, shocked exhalation escaping dry lips.

He'd been dreaming again, the same dream he had every time he slept. In it, he was hopeless and helpless, his body restrained by an unseen force. He stood at the top of the staircase in the house he now claimed as his own. At the bottom of the stairs, standing tall and looking elegant, was his deceased wife Jennifer.

At first she was smiling. An infectious smile that spread a warm sensation through his body. It was a happy smile, a loving smile; he always returned the gesture. They stared at each other for several moments. He was mesmerized by the beauty of her expression.

He tried to walk down the stairs— the urge to touch her and to be with her was overpowering—but he couldn't move. He had no control over his own body. He tried to speak, at first to tell her how much he loved her, but his mouth refused to form any words. In desperation, he tried to call to her, to beckon her to him, but he couldn't.

Panic took over as he tried to understand what was wrong, but before he could reach a conclusion, Jennifer's warm expression changed. Her smile faded, her lips curled. Her loving eyes opened wide in shock and her delicate hands covered her face in horrific anticipation.

In the dream, Lee experienced physical and emotional pain. His heart ached, his head throbbed, and his vision faded just as a dark silhouette emerged behind his wife. He tried to shout. He tried to scream. But when he opened his mouth only air escaped. He wanted to throw himself down the stairs, to launch at the mysterious figure, but his muscles weren't his own.

The darkness enveloped his wife, hovering over her and then swooping down upon her like a lion taking down its prey. He watched, horrified and helpless, as the blackness engulfed her, sucking the life out of her before slowly fading into the nothingness from which it came.

The life had been siphoned out of her, and with tears streaming down his face, Joseph was forced to look upon her lifeless body once more.

He always woke at that point. He had only seen her butchered body for a split second, but it was long enough to burn the tortured image onto his waking mind.

Staring up at the living room ceiling, Joseph Lee contemplated the dream and the night that had led to its inception. Since the death of his wife, he didn't enjoy sleeping and tried his best to avoid it. The night before, he drank to drown his sorrows, of which there were many. By the side of the couch, toppled onto their sides, were two empty bottles of whiskey. He stared at them and instinctively closed his eyes, hoping to banish the piercing migraine the liquor had invited into his head.

He gently massaged his temple, his hand covering his face as his fingers worked. He watched as a faded ray of sunlight danced between the gaps in his fingers. The light had escaped through a crack in the living room curtains, exposing millions of dust particles sitting in the air like distant stars.

He had fallen asleep watching television: a documentary, a film, he wasn't sure, and he hadn't been sure when he was watching it. It was background noise, flashing pictures to entertain a drunken mind and prevent it from digging in on itself and revealing disturbing memories. At some point in the night, he'd woken and turned off the big screen TV. The remote lay by the side of the couch, nestled between a whiskey bottle and the wrapper from a microwave burger.

He rolled off the couch, landing with a soft thump on the padded carpet. Clouds of dust erupted into the air, escaping thick fabric that hadn't felt the touch of a vacuum cleaner in months.

He hadn't done any real cleaning since Jennifer had been murdered. In the months that had followed her death, he had done some erratic housework, cleaning away the scent and sights of death, preoccupying his mind while the police checked and rechecked his house and his statement. Eventually he had given up. There was no point anymore.

He bought everything he needed online and had it delivered to his house. He spent his days watching television, wallowing in self-pity, and filling his time with mundane activities that kept him away from the real world. The few friends he had had stopped visiting and calling months before. The remains of his family—an older brother, a nephew, and a few cousins—had broken off contact with him, despite always being close. He had ceased to exist in the eyes of others. Nothing and no one in the real world wanted him, and he didn't want anyone or anything out there either.

He hadn't left the house in six months.

He slowly clambered to his feet, peeling his face away from the musty carpet and the stale scent that clung to its fibers and his nose. He sluggishly stumbled out of the living room, wincing as his migraine reacted to the movement.

Alive, Jennifer had been a successful lawyer from an equally successful family. Her mother had died three years before her, with her father passing two years before that. They left Jennifer and her sister everything they had worked their lives to achieve: a sizeable wealth that promised an easy life for both of them. Jennifer had shared her wealth with Joseph. He had been a nobody when she fell in love with him, and he remained a nobody throughout their relationship, but she supported him.

Her money was now his money, passed down via two generations of success, to a third generation of nothing. It meant he would never have to work a day in his life. For that, he was lucky, but not thankful. He didn't want money; he didn't care about material wealth. He'd lost the only person he'd loved. Now he had nothing.

He cringed as his bare feet slapped against the hallway's wooden floors, which led from the front door, around the staircase, and into the kitchen. He paused in the middle of the hallway, the staircase to his left. His eyes traced an invisible pattern on the hardwood floor, and unwanted memories found their way back into his tired mind.

The front door rattled behind him and he almost jumped out of his skin. With his heart pounding aggressively, he stared at the front entrance. Through the door's glass panel, he could see a short red blur, bobbing impatiently as it waited.

The blur knocked on the door again, four knocks, each louder than the last. He waited for his breathing to slow and his heart to steady before approaching the door.

He opened it slowly and with a great degree of caution. He squinted through the morning light, staring at the stubby figure of a delivery driver who was smiling at him through thick-rimmed spectacles, his chubby cheeks dimpled.

"Hi there." Despite the early hour and the grumpy man in front of him, the delivery driver seemed to be in a pleasant mood. He held a brown package, which he offered to Joseph. "Could you take this parcel in for number twenty-three please?" The driver phrased as a question, but it looked like he'd already decided upon the answer. He was ready to back away, to leave the parcel and the responsibility, and to get on with his round.

Lee stared disinterestedly at the package. "Why?" he said warily.

"They're not in." He flashed a wide smile. He waited for Lee to respond and spoke again when he didn't. "I've been knocking on the door for the last few minutes. They're either asleep and ignoring me or they're at work." He chuckled.

Lee gave him an apathetic glare.

"I tried their next-door neighbors," he continued. "They must be at work, too."

Joseph nodded unenthusiastically. "I don't know them," he said blankly. "What's their name?" He grabbed the package, read the name, and then handed it back to the flabbergasted man. "What kind of name is that? I can barely even read it."

"It's German, I believe."

"Do you speak German?"

"No," the delivery man said, somewhat taken aback.

"Have you been to Germany?"

"Well, no."

"Then how would you know?"

"It's just a guess." His smile had faded, replaced with a look of bemusement.

"Have you met them before?"

"Well, no, I've—"

Lee sighed. "If I take this parcel, I'm obliged to go around to their house later on and give it to them?"

"Well, yes."

"You want me to take time out of my day to speak to people I've never met?" Lee's eyebrows were raised.

The man retreated slightly, defeated. "Look, if you don't want to take it, that's fine."

Lee faked a burst of laughter. "I'm only messing with you," he said, grinning.

The smile returned to the face of the chubby delivery man and he proffered the package again. "So you'll take it then?"

"No." Lee shut the door, a fake grin still etched on his face. Through the pane glass, he saw the red blob back up, turn, and then walk away.

He didn't want to associate with his neighbors. He hadn't done so while Jennifer was alive and he didn't want to buck the trend now she was dead. They all knew about her death. It didn't matter whether they'd actually met her or not, gossip had a way of spreading its evil tongue through suburban streets and poisoning everyone in its wake. And Lee was at the head of that gossip—the source of their hatred and the target for their anger.

3

In his studio, on the second floor of his three-story home, Joseph Lee sat in silence, his mind elsewhere, his eyes fixed on a blank canvas. The studio had been built for him. Initially it had been a spare bedroom, dark, unwelcoming and good for storage only. Jennifer had used her money and her flair for interior decorating to change that, knocking down walls, putting in windows, and creating a spacious, bright, and welcoming room where her husband could spend any creative energy he found.

He hadn't found any of that energy for nearly a year.

He had never thought of himself as a particularly gifted man, but he had a wild imagination. His only true talent, although he refused to accept it as such, came through a series of creative outlets. One of which was painting.

As a child, he'd had a gift for sketching. In school, he was considered a less than average student. He never paid attention to the teachers, tended not to socialize, and spent the majority of his time doodling and daydreaming. The doodling progressed to painting when he hit his teens and culminated with him enrolling in an art class at his local college.

It didn't turn out the way he hoped. Instead of being a gateway into a possible career, it became a dead-end annoyance. He couldn't adhere to set rules, wasn't interested in learning about the science of painting—of lights and angles—and he had no interest in painting live models. He saw art as a way to vent his emotions and let his mind venture from the rigors of life. He dropped the class, but not before it changed his life.

He'd met Jennifer in college. She was teaching a part-time course in English Literature—open to the public, operated by volunteers. Poetry was one of her many loves, and this allowed her to express her adoration. He still had fond memories of her at the head of the class, a grin on her face and a passion in her voice as she recited the classics.

Joseph stabbed his finger into a fresh batch of sunset yellow and flicked it absently at the canvas. He always refilled his palettes with fresh paint when he entered the studio, but he hadn't used them properly in a long time. What he created was no longer art. At best, he was dirtying the canvas, wasting paper and paint.

He had met Jennifer in the lunch room, instantly signing up to her course so he could see more of her. It wasn't the first time he'd written poetry, but it was the first time he had let others read it. Poetry was another outlet of his and, coupled with his talent for painting and the charm he possessed in his younger days, it had been more than enough to win over the full-time law student and part-time poet.

The paint dried quickly on the canvas, forming a nasty yellow crust. It looked like a small animal had vomited on the paper.

After dating Jennifer, Joseph began to share her interest in writing. He wrote more poetry and even the occasional short story. He enjoyed her delighted expressions when she read his work more than he enjoyed writing it.

Turning his attention away from the messy canvas, he trailed his eyes lazily across the room. The walls, once filled with his artwork, were bare. In his early days, he had painted portraits of Jennifer, capturing every angle and expression. She was so full of life, so radiant and so beautiful, and he painted her as he saw her. His art turned to different topics as their relationship grew, but he still liked to be surrounded by paintings of her.

He had removed the artwork from the walls many months ago, locking them away in the attic. They were reminders of something he wanted to forget. In years to come, he hoped he could look fondly on them again, but as long as they broke his heart, as long as they triggered more bad memories than good, they would continue to gather dust.

He kicked his heels against the floor and rolled the chair across the room, its wheels leaving tracks on the dusty hardwood. He stopped at the expansive windows, pressing his feet against the low sills to stop the momentum. The windows let in more light than Lee wanted to see, more of the real world than he wanted to acknowledge. It had been Jennifer's idea to install the low-hanging windows, one of the first things she focused on during the renovation. She thought the light and the view would inspire him. Lee disagreed, but he had kept his thoughts to himself.

Through the windows, he could see his own front garden in its entirety, as well as the gardens of two neighbors opposite. The lack of maintenance had turned his garden into a mess of tall grass and thick weeds, topped with a layer of dead leaves. In comparison, the garden opposite and to the left was an Eden, with brightly bloomed flower beds wrapped around a neatly trimmed lawn. The second garden, directly opposite, was still recovering from the harsh winter. The grass had been neglected for months, the flowers lay dying in their pots and baskets.

He kicked off the wall, spun the chair backward. He grabbed the easel to steady himself, looked from the filled palette to the easel and back again. The brushes lay next to it, all lined up in order, from largest to smallest, thinnest to thickest, separated in two columns on a well-worn wooden stand.

All the brushes were clean and bone dry.

After several hours of staring at the canvas, with few thoughts running though his tired mind and with the sun painting an ever-retreating shadow on the studio floor, Joseph Lee gave up.

4
—

L ee scribbled lazily at a three-week-old mega-crossword
he'd discovered in the local bi-monthly paper. The A4
pages were filled with advertisements of local businesses,
numerous readers' letters on uninteresting local events, and a
few badly written articles. He had found it stuffed underneath
the sofa, torn and tatty.

His mind had become preoccupied with trying to keep itself
occupied. His wandering hands had dug out the paper and a
pen with the unenthusiastic intention of reading it, doodling
on blank spots, or simply staring at the pictures. The editor's
picture in the back was just about to receive a pen mustache
when he spotted the crossword. He was so distant he hadn't
managed to find a single clue. He found himself reading the
same line over and over, never quite grasping just what it was
saying.

The television played to an uninterested host. Evening was
about to break; the streams of children's television on the major
terrestrial channels was finishing. The mindless chat-shows,
family-friendly game shows, and lifestyle programs were all
making way for the news; a break in the schedule, padding for
primetime.

He had watched a lot of television since his wife's death, yet he hadn't really seen any of the programs. It was just background noise. He didn't bother to channel surf anymore, barely using the hundreds of channels his satellite service offered. Occasionally he tuned into the documentary or movie channels, but his usual preference was to just turn on the set and leave it on. If it distracted him for ten minutes, it was worth it.

He discarded the newspaper and rolled over on the couch, his head buried into the thick fabric. He stayed there for several minutes, almost falling asleep, drifting in and out of brief dreams, until a soft thumping alerted him. Someone was at the door.

He let the unknown caller knock again, sinking his head further into the thick cushion as three knocks, each louder than the last, echoed throughout the house and drummed into his conscious.

He listened to the silence that followed the knocks. He could hear voices other than those coming from the television, where a well-mannered newscaster refreshed the public on the latest atrocities.

Three more knocks, louder and more urgent.

Lee sighed into the cushion and pushed himself up, first to his knees, then lazily to his feet. He plodded to the door, where two blurred figures waited on the other side.

"Who is it?" he half-shouted, half-mumbled, his voice heavy with fatigue.

The two people on the other side of the door confided with each other before one of them, a man, answered, "The Lechnen's. We're your new neighbors."

Lee frowned, rolled his eyes. He opened the door and instantly greeted the callers with squinted eyes and a creased brow. "What do you wa—" he paused, his words catching in his throat.

"I'm Riso," the man stated proudly, noticing that Lee's attention was on his wife. "This is my wife, Zala," he explained, content to let Lee stare.

"Hello," Zala said, smiling at the transfixed Joseph Lee, a touch of shyness in her smile.

"*Jennifer,*" Lee stuttered, his voice a whisper.

"Excuse me?" Riso said, smiling the broad smile of a simpleton.

Lee turned to the man, as though noticing him for the first time. "Nothing," he said quickly. Turning back to the woman he added: "You just surprised me."

She smiled broadly, a sight which stirred something deep within Lee. He stared at her in admiration and amazement. She was the double of his wife. It was like staring into his past or relenting to his graphic nightmares.

Her blue eyes twinkled with a beauty Lee had only ever witnessed in the eyes of his wife. Her features were warm, soft, beautiful. She had a bright, confident, and reassuring smile, the same smile that had kept Lee content throughout his relationship.

"I do apologize if we startled you," Riso said genuinely. His English was strong and well pronounced, his accent noticeable only on certain syllables.

"No, it's okay," Lee said, more inclined to talk. "I don't get many visitors, that's all. My name's Joseph by the way, Joseph Lee." The friendly foreigner extended a hand, which Lee shook hesitantly. "So . . . " He found his eyes constantly drifting to Zala's inviting smile. "You're new around here?"

"Yes," they both said in unison, smiling like newsreaders.

"We moved here last week," Riso said, glancing at his wife.

Zala nodded. "It's a very quiet neighborhood, one of the reasons we moved here," she added. Joseph watched her lips intently as she spoke, even though her voice was subtle and mellow, Lee found it odd to hear such harsh accentuated words coming from her mouth. He almost expected her to speak like Jennifer.

"It is not too friendly, though," Riso said, breaking a brief silence, the awkwardness of which was apparent to them but lost on Lee. "We were expecting maybe a few welcome parties but none of the neighbors have been to see us." A note of sadness coated his words.

Lee nodded. *"Set of bastards,"* he said placidly and without thought.

"Excuse me?"

He studied his new neighbor. He was tall and broad and had a posture to match. He stood up perfectly straight, as if standing to attention. His wide shoulders were pushed back, his arms stretched by his sides, and despite being a few inches taller than Lee, his head was perfectly straight. Instead of adjusting his neck to look into Joseph's gaze, he simply lowered his eyes, almost squinting.

"Where are you from?" Lee wondered. He became conscious of the fact that he was staring at Zala. He forced his gaze to swap between the couple, flicking it back and forth like a spectator at a slow tennis game.

"Greenwich," Riso said simply.

Lee nodded slowly, waited for further clarification and then spoke again when he received none. "I mean *initially*, are you German?"

"Ah," Riso grinned. "We are from Austria." He looked across at his wife. "We moved to England nearly ten years ago."

Lee nodded and smiled but didn't reply. He let a few more awkward moments drift by, less aware of it than they were as he waited for them to get to the point.

"Oh!" Riso barked, "How silly of me, I almost forgot why we came here. I think you have a parcel for us?"

Lee simply shook his head.

The two Austrians looked at each other. Their smiles vanished as they exchanged confused gazes, only to reappear when they turned back to Lee.

"The delivery driver said he had left it with a neighbor?" Riso offered. "He left a note . . . " he allowed the sentence to trail off.

"He didn't leave it with me."

"Everyone else seems to be at work," Zala spoke again, much to Joseph's delight. "This is a very busy neighborhood."

"They're all at work," Lee explained. "That's the problem with deliveries, they can only drop off the parcels during *their* work hours, which just so happens to be everyone else's work hours. You think they'd start delivering on a Sunday or at night, it would be easier for them, there'd be less traffic on the roads, the companies could employ more people because no one works on a Sunday and it seems everyone wants a second job nowadays. . . and every house they knocked on would actually answer," he explained tiresomely, stopping to take note of their expressions. He'd expected baffled or bored features but instead they seemed to be smiling even more than before.

Riso laughed boorishly, "You're a wise man," he said cheerfully.

"Uh huh," Lee said in a hushed and puzzled voice. "Which house do you live in?" he questioned, popping his head outside and looking around the street to add emphasis to his question.

"House 23," Zala said softly, hooking a thumb over her shoulder. "Just opposite."

"Did you know the previous owner?" Riso quizzed quickly.

"I never paid much attention to the neighbors. Like you said, they're busy all the time."

"We are not," Riso exclaimed. "I have a few weeks away from work in fact, to help settle in the house." He paused, his expression filled with thought. "Why don't you come across later on? I was planning to get out the barbecue, open a few cans, and test out our new garden furniture."

Lee recoiled from the invite, his actions spoke louder than words.

Zala quickly said, "We'd love to have you over."

"You'd be our first guest," Riso added. He and his wife had now locked arms, both of their smiling faces were aimed at Joseph Lee. "We're neighbors now. We should eat and drink together, yes?"

Lee's face cringed with a mixture of distaste and apprehension; he struggled to find a good lie but their smiling faces forced his mouth to say something his mind didn't want to. "Sure, why not."

"Excellent," Riso proclaimed. "Come around later on tonight. We'll look forward to it!" He extended an arm.

Lee faked a smile and accepted the handshake.

"Now I guess we have to go knocking on neighbors' doors to find our parcel!" Riso said merrily.

"Yeah, good luck with that."

"We will see you later, Mr. Lee."

Lee caught Zala's smile before the couple turned to leave. He didn't want to socialize, no matter how friendly the company was, but he had a feeling Zala would make things more interesting for him.

5

―

The washing machine purred for the first time in months. A collection of clothes bundled around at high speed, passing through jets of hot water as the entire appliance rocked, sending volts of vibrations into the floor. The spinning clothes were watched by absent eyes.

Visions of Jennifer Lee flashed into Joseph's mind. He pictured her smiling in the heat of the Caribbean sun, her head resting on a cushion of her own lustrous hair as she reclined on a sun chair, watching the blue skies above and enjoying the peace.

He remembered the smiles of enchantment that lit up her face when she first saw the streams of artwork he had devoted to her. The feigned grin of disinterest as she listened to his absurd, drunken conspiracy theories. He even remembered the times she cried: the death of her parents, the loss of a pet—one cat and two goldfish, the former had eaten the latter—an angry argument, or a sad film.

He replayed the memories together with the fresh images of his neighbor. He felt like he saw Jennifer every day—her face was always in his thoughts, in his dreams and on photographs hidden in drawers—but seeing her again, in the flesh, felt otherworldly. Only it was someone else's flesh.

He'd never felt like he needed or wanted to move on. He had only ever loved one woman and she was gone. Everyone else that followed would only be walking in her footsteps. But after seeing Zala, his thoughts shifted.

The washing machine beeped three times. Joseph glared at it. The water had stopped flowing, the clothes had stopped spinning. The machine beeped again, one long head-churning noise.

"What?" Lee asked the idle machine. It had taken him twenty minutes to figure out how to turn it on. He wasn't interested in learning its language.

Since Jennifer's death, he preferred to buy new clothes instead of trying to wash his old ones, but lately he hadn't bothered to do either. He wanted to look his best when meeting his new neighbors, not for social or cleanliness sake, just for Zala.

He jabbed at the buttons across the top of the machine, eventually finding the right one. He removed the sodden clothes and scooped them into his arms, clutching them against his naked torso and then dropping them into the dryer.

After a few minutes, with sensations of cold pricking at his skin and lifting the hairs on his arms, the dryer whirled into action and Lee retreated to his thoughts again, his arms folded over his chest to keep out the cold.

———

From the wide windows inside the brightly lit studio, Lee watched as clouds of smoke pushed their way into the evening air from the Lechnens' house. He couldn't see the back garden from where he sat, but he saw a mass of lights shining out from its direction. It looked like the majority of the lights inside the house were also on.

When the smoke emerged from over the top of the house, Lee made his way downstairs. The new neighbors hadn't specified a time and he'd found himself in an awkward position, nervous for the first time in a long time. He didn't want to go over too early. If he did and they hadn't set up the barbecue, they would then feel obliged to do so. He also didn't want to leave it too late and find himself knocking on the front door with no one to answer because they were around the back listening to music and enjoying themselves.

He hadn't realized how much of a social outcast he had become until that moment. He had never had the social touch, but in the past he'd never really cared. He had always had a subtle confidence that came from a total lack of respect and complete indifference to his surroundings.

Standing at his own front door, his heart beating fast, his palms sweaty, Joseph Lee pondered.

Should I take something? he wondered. *A bottle of wine, a few cans.* He scuttled into the kitchen and opened the drinks cabinet. A half empty bottle of cheap vodka sat solitary in the middle. In the fridge, he found two cans of lager, with the top of one coated in a congealed substance that had dripped down from the shelf above. He examined the substance and instantly recoiled. On the shelf above, he found the stinky culprit, a block of cheese three months past its sell-by date. It had turned a putrid shade of green and seemed to be growing hair. He wiped the cheese juice from the top of the can, but couldn't rid it of its rancid stench.

He decided against a housewarming gift and left the house after throwing on a leather jacket. The street was silent except for the house the new neighbors occupied. Lights from living rooms beamed through closed blinds and drawn curtains, flickering occasional blue streams. The stench of flame-grilled meat, accompanied by the sounds of soft pop music, floated across the road, polluting the night air and tingling Lee's taste buds.

Walking down the garden path to number 23, he studied his surroundings. The garden was neglected, covered with dead leaves and dying flowers, although it was nowhere near as bad as Lee's own garden. They seemed like people who would take pride in appearances. Lee assumed they would have the garden looking like a wonderland within a week or two.

Parked in the gravel driveway was an immaculately clean Mercedes. The glare of the streetlight allowed Lee to catch a glimpse of his reflection on its polished surface. He watched his own distorted mirror image as it bounced down the pathway to the front door and raised a fist to the wood.

After half a dozen knocks, a small spotlight above the door burst into life, showering Lee with a bright white glow. He lowered his hand and blinked away the beam. Seconds later, the handle turned and Zala Lechnen appeared.

"Mr. Lee," she said excitedly. "You came! *Excellent!*" She shifted aside to allow Joseph past. "Please, come in."

"Thank you," he muttered softly. "And please, call me Joseph."

He crossed the threshold in slow motion. When he passed within inches of Zala, their eyes met, their faces a mere foot apart. Lee's nostrils tingled, his smile faltered. He could feel her warmth and sense her body as he brushed against her. He breathed her in and reveled in her aura as his heart pounded so loud he worried she would hear it.

The moment was over quickly, leaving Lee to realize that he hadn't been that close to another human being in a long time.

Zala carefully closed the door behind him and walked down the corridor. She ushered for Lee to follow her as she strolled gracefully across the laminated floor.

"You came just in time," she said over her shoulder. "Riso was just putting the meat on the barbecue."

Lee nodded and watched the swaying hips of the look-alike. She wore light, loose-fitting clothes; her white blouse swayed gently around her torso as she walked. Gray jogging pants flapped at her naked ankles, flicking the tops of her bare feet and picking up flecks of dust from the floor.

"I hope you like a drink." She crossed into the kitchen and made for the patio door at the back end of the house.

"I do, yes," Lee said politely.

"You'll be in good company here then."

She stepped through the opening in the patio door and toward a pair of flip-flops waiting on the deck. Joseph could see the streams of smoke coming from the side of the garden, panning out from a barbecue. He watched her slide into the flip-flops, his own feet still inside the confines of the house.

"No need to wait for me," she said, smiling. "You are quite the gentleman, aren't you?"

Lee smiled. "I guess so." If anything, it was because he was shy and lost, his mind rampant with random thoughts, his body stuck as if waiting for orders, his hands stuffed into his pockets like an idle teen.

With her feet ensconced, Zala stepped forward and hooked her arm through Lee's. She smiled at him. "Come on then, gentleman," she said jokingly. "Escort me to the barbecue."

Joseph couldn't help but smile. Immediately his anxiety softened and the tension in his body vanished. He returned her smile, her breath on his lips as he faced her. "Yes, my lady."

———

Two sets of garden furniture sat on top of a stone deck that overlooked a bland and colorless garden that suffered the same misfortune and neglect as the front. The food and drink on offer more than made up for the bland surroundings.

Lee and Zala sat on wooden chairs in front of a large round table. Two other chairs occupied the table, but no one occupied them. In the middle of this table were plates and bowls of various offerings, including buttered bread buns and a bowl of potato salad, which nestled in the middle of an encirclement of crisps, rice, relish, and peanuts.

Riso grabbed Lee a can of beer from an icebox immediately after greeting him, insisting he drink straight away.
Zala, sitting next to Lee and sharing his view of the garden,
held a tall glass of white wine in her hand, with the open bottle sitting on the table in front of her. Next to this table was
another, which stood beside the smoking barbecue, a large
chrome device holding vast quantities of meat on three separate cooking shelves. Rio seemed to be in his element as he
operated it, grinning through the thick smoke and talking
over the hiss of the sizzling meat. Between breaks of billow-
ing smoke, with sweat beads popping on his forehead and
smoke stinging his eyes, he drank thirstily from a beer glass
the size of a vase.

Lee had been at the house less than two minutes and had
spoken nothing more than a few greetings, but already he felt
calm and welcomed.

"I hope you like meat," Riso shouted.

Lee looked at the steaming grill. He could smell a range of
burgers, chops, and hotdogs sizzling away. "I do," he replied
with a smile. "But that's a lot of food. Are you expecting more
people, a pack of wolves maybe?"

Riso laughed his boorish laugh and took another long drink
of beer. "You are our first guest and this is our first barbecue in
our new house, so I thought, *why not make it special?*"

"Makes sense."

"Anything that doesn't get eaten, we can give to the dogs."

Lee looked around. "You have a dog?"

"No," Riso said grinning. "I was hoping *you* did!"

They all laughed, chipping further away at ice that had
already been broken.

The barbecue hissed violently, spilling more swarms of
heavy smoke. Riso backed away, waiting for the thick clouds
to dissipate.

Zala turned to Joseph, a loving smile etched on her soft face. "I hope you like your meat burned."

"I don't mind." Lee smiled. "That's one hell of a beast." He gestured toward the barbecue, a volcano spewing plumes to the fading day.

"The barbecue or Riso?"

"I heard that!" Riso called, his laugh lingering on his lips. "I got this thing a few months ago," he called through the thick smoke. "It's a beauty, isn't it? I can grill up to twenty burgers at once on this."

Lee's eyebrows arched, and he thought about questioning the Austrian giant but decided against it.

"He never *has* and he never *will*," Zala said, reading Lee's expression. "We're not ones for huge parties or social gatherings. *Although*, if it wasn't for me, I'm sure he'd cook up the burgers and eat them all himself."

"Of course!" Riso said over the top of his beer glass. "I love my meat!"

Lee nodded. Riso certainly looked like a man who enjoyed his meat; his heavy physique had clearly seen a lot of protein over the years.

Zala shook her head at her husband's reaction. "It's a good thing he works out so much," she told Lee, her eyes on her husband. "If he didn't exercise all that congealed fat out of his veins, he'd be dead by now."

Riso frowned.

"I keep telling him to watch what he eats," she said distantly, turning away from her husband and looking directly into Lee's eyes. "So, Joseph . . . " She spoke his name with a soft subtlety, her accent disappearing for those two syllables. "What do you do?"

He looked at her over the rim over his glass and raised his eyebrows. "Do?" he asked, taking a mouthful of ice-cold beer.

"Where do you work?" she reiterated, quickly adding, "if you don't mind me asking."

Lee did mind. He hadn't worked on a decent lie and he wasn't ready to tell strangers about the entirety of his jobless life and how he came by his huge fortune, no matter how welcoming they were. "I paint and write mostly," he said, realizing that if he provided enough information, relevant or not, he may be able to sidestep around the word *job*.

"I do it all at home. I have a studio on the second floor—big, bright, empty. You've probably seen it from outside. The windows are huge. It's like a conservatory up there." He took a sip of his drink with the implied expression that more information was to come, which he hoped he could think of during the short pause. "Painting is my strong point. I do the occasional portrait and landscape, but most of what I paint comes from within, I guess. I also do a bit of poetry and prose; I haven't gone as far to write a novel yet but I have completed a few short stories and poetry anthologies." He paused again, realizing that both of the Lechnens were staring at him with great interest.

He felt a nervousness creep over him. He didn't like being the center of attention. "I have many creative outlets," he continued, rushed. "That's what Jennifer always used to say—" he paused, his heart skipping a few beats. He hadn't wanted to bring her up.

"Is Jennifer your wife?" Zala quizzed.

"*Was*," Lee said quickly, choosing to take another drink and a subsequent break from the conversation. "We . . . broke up. A while ago."

"Oh, I'm so sorry." He spotted a genuine sympathetic flicker in her blue eyes.

"It's okay," Joseph feigned a smile. "We didn't work well together."

"Women!" Riso shouted brashly. His tone, just like his laugh, carried an unintended abrasiveness to it. "You can't live with them and you can't get laid without them!" He began to laugh but his wife stopped him with a stern look.

Lee smiled, content. "So, what do you two do?" he asked politely, happy the conversation was moving away from him.

"Have you heard of August Transport?" Riso wondered.

"Sure," Lee lied.

"I own the place," Riso said proudly. "It's a family business. I came over here from Austria ten years ago to help my uncle run the company—back then we only had two depots, now we have seven all over the country, with more in the pipeline." He stepped away from the smoke, moving closer to Lee, the vase of beer in his hand.

"In Austria, I was a soldier, I joined the army when I left school and spent the best days of my life there. I always knew I'd have the family business to fall back on so I was free to see the world and I didn't have to worry about the shitty paycheck the army gave me." He paused to take a drink, simultaneously rubbing his smoke-peppered eyes. "I left not long after I met Zala." He nodded toward his wife, as if Lee needed verification. "The army is no place for a married man."

"You were getting old and tired, that's why you left," Zala joked.

"True," Riso agreed with another burst of harsh laughter. "Zala works there too." Again he pointed at his wife, his thick finger peeling away from the cold glass. "Well, she's on the books anyway." He winked before downing the remaining beer, swallowing half a pint of the dark liquid in two big gulps.

"Drink up, Joseph!" he exclaimed merrily. "I drank two cans before you got here. You have some catching up to do!"

———

Joseph Lee stumbled out of the Lechnen house a few hours later, his merry feet treading the tarmac of the quiet street, the intoxicated Austrians shouting their good-byes behind him.

"It was great having you over," the voice of Riso Lechnen boomed, no doubt waking up a few annoyed neighbors.

His wife, standing next to him and swaying gently with an absent smile on her face, hushed her husband. "Sleep well," she said in a softer tone.

Lee waved a final good-bye to his new friends and made his way across the street, fumbling in his pockets for his front door key.

The neighborhood was asleep, living room lights no longer ablaze. Three houses down, Lee saw an upstairs light burst into life out of the corner of his blurred vision, but he paid it no heed. The neighbors were too private and retiring to complain about anything. A few loud noises in the night certainly wouldn't upset them.

It had been a fun night. He had enjoyed himself for the first time in a long time, his troubles melted away under the welcoming pressure of alcohol and pleasant conversation. After cooking up enough meat to feed an army, half of which had been wrapped in foil and placed in the fridge for a later date, Riso joined Lee and his wife at the table. They consumed vast amounts of alcohol, talked about anything and everything. The conversation had flowed with effortless ease.

With every bottle of beer, the conversation had both broadened and dimmed somewhat, from views about politics, modern art, and classic literature to outlandish jokes and nonsensical opinions, putting the world to rights.

Much to Lee's delight, Zala had stayed in touch with the conversation, her mind just as broad and her opinions just as crazy. She also joined in when the discussions moved onto sports.

At the end of the night, Riso opened a bottle of vodka he had been saving for *special occasions*, claiming that the beginning of a new friendship couldn't be more special. He lined up shots on the table and the three drank with great thirst and joy, cheering one another on like partying students.

Joseph Lee stumbled into his house. His eyes instinctively fell to the laminated floor, tracing over an invisible outline as they always did, but for the first time, his heart didn't sink. His face was a picture of happiness, accentuated with a broad smile that stretched from ear to ear.

Stumbling into the living room, not bothering to switch on the lights, he collapsed onto the sofa, sunk his head into the cushions, and closed his eyes. Memories of his happy night flashed and spun through the blackness, a carnival behind closed shutters. In less than five minutes, still smiling like a simpleton, he was asleep.

———

When he awoke and his tired mind tuned into the world, it noticed something different; something odd. He was hungover, that wasn't much of a surprise; his dehydrated brain had shriveled to an unhealthy size, compliments to the foreign beer and expensive vodka, but the dry lips and throbbing head didn't bother him.

His mood was different, lighter. He even managed a smile whilst he was rubbing his eyes—an involuntary twinge, a merry tic. Sleep itself was a natural mood lifter and energizer, especially for someone who got very little of it, but Lee rarely felt energized upon waking. Sitting up on the sofa, something quickly dawned on him, as though the blood rush had forced his brain into gear. He hadn't woken with a start. He hadn't dreamed about Jennifer. His sleep had been restful, uninterrupted by the sickening images of her massacred body. He failed to recount *any* dreams. The only memories that offered themselves were of the night before: the beer, the conversation, the meat, the special vodka and, most prominent of all, Zala.

He staggered to the kitchen, flicked on the kettle, and rested against the countertop while it heated up. Despite being the spitting image of Jennifer, Zala Lechnen didn't share many other qualities with Joseph's buried wife. They were both compassionate and loving people, a gorgeous virtue that shone through to their exterior and expressed itself in an unforgettable smile, but the similarities stopped there.

Jennifer was a career-motivated, professional woman. She had an intimidating, powerful demeanor coupled with an assertiveness that tended to overshadow her innocence. She had developed the personality for her work. As a lawyer, she needed an edge; she needed to be ruthless and cold, even if her poetic side didn't agree with it. She was also a workaholic. Joseph would go for days at a time without seeing her, and when he did, he often encountered the cold-hearted Jennifer and not the compassionate one.

In her earlier days, she had always been the innocent *butter wouldn't melt in her mouth* type. As she furthered her career, she worked more hours and lost more innocence, but away from the stresses of work, she still maintained the sensitive mannerisms that warmed Lee's heart.

Zala's personality hadn't seen the likes of such a stressful job. She had never had to feign heartlessness to win a case or intimidate people to get answers. The compassionate side of her personality remained fully intact.

The steam from the kettle rose through the funnelled top and dispersed as it collided with the base of a protruding cupboard. Lee watched the dispersing fog inattentively.

There was still a lot about Zala that he didn't know, and every part of him yearned to learn. Listening to her last night, he had discovered many things that surprised and delighted him. Her married life had been simple. She was a housewife who hadn't worked since her teenage years. She had no children to look after and, other than making Riso's tea when he arrived back from work, she had no major chores. She had the makings of a woman whose personality and purpose had been stomped out by a macho man with archaic designs on life and feminism. But she was independent, she was strong, and while Riso made many jokes suggesting otherwise, he was not a chauvinist, and he didn't keep his wife under lock and key.

Zala spoke fluent English and Spanish and had her mind set on learning Portuguese. Through home-learning courses, she had achieved diplomas in English literature, social sciences, and psychology and would begin studying toward a Psychology degree next year. She could play the piano—Lee had been treated to a short, sweet, and drunken recital—and she was a big film buff.

She also had an interest in art and had asked to see Lee's paintings many times during the night. He had side-stepped the question with modesty at first, but he relented eventually, making a promise that he didn't really want to keep.

He wasn't sure if he was infatuated with her, but he was certainly mesmerized by her. His current mental state didn't call for a relationship of any kind—he could barely handle any human contact—but he enjoyed Zala's company, and not just because she reminded him of Jennifer. After all, he had gone out of his way to remove any reminders of Jennifer from his house and his mind.

He poured himself a black coffee loaded with three sugars and then climbed the stairs and entered the studio. He glanced blankly at the easel and canvas, the centerpiece of the room, before settling down onto the swivel chair and rolling it to the expansive windows.

Pushing his feet against the wall, he allowed the chair to recline as far as it would go as he sipped the bitter black liquid and stared at the Lechnen's house. He stared intently at the closed curtains on the second floor, beyond which lay the master bedroom. He imagined Zala lying in bed, covered with the flimsy material of a silk nightdress and wrapped snug in a thick duvet, her sweet eyes closed, the innocence of sleep pressed onto her soft face.

He pictured her like he remembered Jennifer: her thick hair sprawled on the pillow, her lips gently open. Lost in the lust-filled thoughts, he nearly dropped his coffee when the curtains were suddenly yanked open.

The fantasy of the sleeping beauty disappeared. She had awoken. Holding both ends of the curtains, Zala closed her eyes, sucking in a morning breath and soaking up the sunshine. Her once perfectly straight hair had been ravaged by sleep. Strands of it grasped at her neck and face. She wore a loose green tank top, the right strap had fallen away from her pale neck and wrapped slackly around her arm. Lee imagined nipples poking through the material but, due to the distance between the houses, he saw nothing more than a Zala-shaped blur.

He took a long drink of the scalding coffee and found himself wishing he had a pair of binoculars, a wish that soon disturbed him. He turned his eyes away from the window and shook his head, trying to push the thought away. He didn't want to lust after a married woman, and she was too much like Jennifer.

He finished his coffee with his chair facing the other way as unwanted thoughts raced through his head. He decided to shower; his clothes stank of sweat and alcohol and for the first time in a long time, it actually bothered him.

6

L ee was hungry but there was nothing to eat. With the television blaring out destructive noises from the living room, he stuck his head in the fridge and rummaged around. He rarely ate, and what he did eat came in ready-made packages from the supermarket or from cans that had been in his cupboard for months.

In a cupboard above the sink, he found three cans of beans, a few cans of soup, and a dented can of sweetcorn. In the fridge, he searched the many drawers and compartments. It was a huge contraption, fit for a large and ravenous family, but wasted on a man who ate like a hamster.

He was excited when he found two microwaveable burgers. Opening one, choosing to ignore the use-by date, he popped it in the microwave and waited impatiently as the red digits on the display counted down. He always ate fast food, and he ate it fast. Everyone seemed to do the same; in a world of nonstop work, people needed fast food and they needed it on the go, but Lee barely moved. To him, food wasn't something to be enjoyed, just as much as a breath of air or a glass of water wasn't to be enjoyed. It was a necessity.

Gunshots and mortar fire erupted from the television, echoing into the kitchen. One of the terrestrial channels he enjoyed so little was showing a war movie from the sixties. It was background noise and company; he didn't care if the company was Nazis or *Tom and Jerry*.

When the microwave pinged, he removed the burger and quickly recoiled from the heat, pulling his hands away. The rubbery slab of beef-like product shot out from between the bread, flew across the room like a Frisbee, and landed with a splat on the floor, the noise coinciding with an exploding grenade from the unwatched television.

He glared momentarily at the circle of suspect meat. He removed it from the floor, inspected the damage, and then began to pick off the various bits of fluff, grit, and dust that had stuck to its surface. After placing the slab back inside the bun, he left it on the countertop, stood back, and stared at it with deep thought and disgust, like a piece of controversial modern art.

There was another one in the fridge, but he was hoping to eat that later. He was hungry—a normal hangover behavior. That side-effect had vanished over the last few months, but it was making a return. Whether it was because he felt happier about himself or because his alcohol consumption had been social and not just a depressing drink to drown his sorrows, he wasn't sure.

He lifted the bun, poured a complementary sachet of sauce over the meat, and contemplated further. Just as he was about to dig in, someone knocked on the door. He glared at the burger one last time before retreating to the door. He needed to place an order with the supermarket, have them deliver some more food. As he made his way to the door, part of him hoped he'd done just that in a drunken haze. He prayed it was the delivery man at his door, carrying bags of prepaid, forgotten food.

He pulled open the door and smiled at the visitor. It wasn't food. It was something far better.

"Zala." He failed to hide or suppress his surprise.

"Hello, Joseph." Zala seemed happy to see him.

"What brings you here?"

She was holding a glass bowl, the top of which had been wrapped in foil. "We had so much food left over from last night." She offered him the bowl. "I wondered if you would want any. You seemed to enjoy it last night . . . " She allowed the sentence to trail off, the bowl proffered in her extended arms.

Lee couldn't help but grin. "You read my mind." As he took it, the scent of meat leaked through the foil and made his mouth water. "Thanks."

"No problem." She turned around to glance at her house before dragging her attention back to him. "I was wondering . . . " she began, unsure how to phrase her words. "Riso is busy doing some work this morning. He might not get any time off work after all. The manager is sick, they are having problems. He may have to go back and help them out. He is the boss after all." She sighed.

"No rest for the wicked, eh?"

Zala nodded. "We were going to go into town today, have a look at the shops and get something to eat at a café or restaurant. Considering he is going to be busy, I was wondering . . . would you like to join me instead?"

Lee was surprised by the request. "Now?"

"Soon, yes. If that's okay. If you'd prefer to go later that would be fine." She seemed to be embarrassed by her request. "Unless you don't want to go at all, of course," she added with a nervous laugh. "I don't mind."

"I'd love to go." Lee grinned. "It's a long walk, do you drive?" Jennifer's Porsche was still parked in the garage, gathering dust along with a small hatchback she used as a run-around, but Lee had never gotten his license.

Zala looked relieved. "Yes, I will drive us there. You will have to show me around, of course. We would be lost otherwise."

"Anywhere particular in mind?" Lee's saliva increased as he spoke, the smell from the meat in his hands wreaking havoc on his empty stomach.

"Not really. I just want to get out of the house and have a look around town. I won't drag you into any clothing stores, I promise."

"I'll hold you to that."

"You can show me some good places, yes?"

"Of course, I've lived here for years." He didn't mention that he had only been downtown a handful of times and never in the last year.

"I'll tell Riso and get my handbag. You come over when you are ready."

Lee nodded. "See you soon."

7

Lee watched the world float by out the passenger side window of the Lechnens' Mercedes. The drive into town should have taken five minutes, but Zala was taking directions from him and he didn't really know where he was going. He'd missed a few turns and they were now taking the long route.

"I didn't realize it was so far," she said as the car rolled onto a freshly laid road, flanked by rows of houses.

"I think I may have missed a turn or two," he confessed, noting Zala's cheeky smile as he did so. "I'm not with it this morning."

"Still a little hungover?"

"I must be."

The air in the car was thick and warm. Sunlight belted in through the windscreen and heated the leather seats. Zala had turned on the air-conditioning but it had yet to break the seemingly impenetrable warmth. A strong scent of vanilla hung in the balmy air, expelled by a pair of air fresheners that dangled from the rearview mirror, mingling with the sensual odor of Zala's perfume. Lee inhaled deeply through his nose, savoring the warmth and the magical scents, before exhaling slowly and tiredly.

"It was a fun night." Zala's eyes were fixed on the road as she spoke, her hands on the top of the wheel, her face set in complete concentration. "Did you enjoy yourself?"

"Yes," Lee nodded. "I've been busy lately; it was nice to get out for once and let my hair down, so to speak—take a left here." He had found his bearings, content he was no longer leading Zala to the middle of nowhere. "I don't normally speak to the neighbors. I can't remember the last time any of them invited me over." He *could* remember; none of them ever had.

"Are they busy or just unsociable?"

"Both. Either that or they don't like me."

Zala sounded a moan of sympathy. "What's not to like? You're a sweet man."

Those words brought a smile to Lee's face, one that he tried and failed to hide.

"I think they're just unsociable," Zala concluded. "You said you didn't know the man who lived in our house before us?"

Lee shook his head. "Did you?"

"Not really. We spoke, but only briefly. He seemed okay. We asked him about the neighborhood, he said it was peaceful and we wouldn't be disturbed. He wasn't a very talkative man. He seemed to have other things on his mind." She spoke slowly. She was clearly a nervous driver, devoting her full attention to the road, but without wanting to seem antisocial.

Lee looked across at the pretty Austrian. Her posture was rigid, awkward, and as close to the steering wheel as the chair would allow. "Living in a good neighborhood is important to you, isn't it?"

She nodded. "We like peace and we like friendships. That's what communities are all about. Everyone looks out for everyone else and treats them with respect."

"In the old days maybe; everyone looks out for number-one nowadays." Lee's words were bitter. He remembered the resentment he had received from the neighbors after Jennifer's murder. She, unlike Lee, *did* speak to the neighbors. She knew all of their names and spoke regularly with a few of them.

"Unfortunately that's true, although we thought it may be a friendly place to live. It certainly seemed like one. The crime figures are low and the people quiet. We looked at the crime figures. We also drove through here a few times, on Friday nights, on the weekend—just to get a feel for it. Everything seemed peaceful and welcoming."

A swarm of paranoia crept over Joseph and, not for the first time, he found himself wondering if she had heard about his wife's murder. He wondered if they knew but didn't want to mention it. "It *is* peaceful." He spoke slowly, his mind processing difficult thoughts. "How long ago did you begin to scope the place out?" He glanced casually out of the window, listening intently for her answer.

Zala giggled at his choice of words. "A few weeks before we moved in," she said, much to his relief. Jennifer's murder only made the local news and the Lechnens' were living in a different district at the time.

"Riso seems like a loud man who likes to party, but he likes peace just as much as me," Zala continued. "He works too hard to live in a noisy neighborhood. It is a shame it is not so friendly, though. I don't work, I stay at home all day. I was hoping to make a few friends, meet some other housewives. Together we could drink coffee and complain about men." Her eyes briefly skirted across to Lee, her head still fixed dead ahead. "I guess you'll do though," she added with a cheeky smile.

"I could use the company," Lee agreed. "I'm not clued up on housewife talk, though. I'm not sure if I'm up to it."

"It's not so hard." The car rolled onto the main street, and Zala made her way toward a large car park. "We swap some recipes, complain about our husbands and their habits—you can use Riso, he has enough bad habits to share between us both—we share some secrets, maybe watch some daytime

TV—" she paused, her tongue hanging out in deep concentration as she swerved the car into the car park. "Oh, and you have to love Johnny Depp."

Lee considered the criteria as Zala parked the car. "I could go for that. Although I'd have to give the daytime TV a miss. I'm not a fan."

"Nah, me neither, its mind-numbing bullshit. But you love Johnny Depp?" she asked with raised eyebrows.

"Sure, who doesn't?"

"Okay!" Zala gasped as she opened the car door. "You're officially a housewife. You're welcome to come over for a coffee anytime." They both stepped out of the car. Zala squinted away the sunshine and peered at Lee over the top of the Mercedes, the glare on the silver surface lighting up her face. "Are you hungry?"

Joseph's stomach growled in excitement, he hadn't had time to eat any of the leftover meat. "Just a bit."

"Then let's get some food."

———

The small town was bustling with activity; the paths lined with busy pedestrians, some making their way to work, some enjoying a stroll in the sun, most doing some morning shopping. The roads, weaving through the thin streets like snakes in wild grass, were packed with cars driven by stressful drivers looking for the routes out of town and lazy shoppers looking to park directly outside the shops.

Lee felt a growing unease spread through him as he and Zala made their way down the street, edging past the busy pedestrians. The town itself wasn't big, the population scarce, but it welcomed visitors from many neighboring villages. Everyone knew everyone else in a town this small, and Lee feared that someone would recognize him and expose his past to the woman by his side.

"Are you okay?" Zala picking up on the apprehension in his expression and the unease in his footsteps.

"I'm fine," Lee quickly replied.

"You really don't get out much do you?" she smirked, locking her arm through his.

"No." His voice was quiet, almost inaudible.

"What do you fancy?" she asked merrily. "A sandwich, some toast, or a full greasy fry-up? I know you English men like your fry-ups."

Joseph felt his stomach rumble in anticipation. "A fry-up sounds good right now. I'm not too fussy, so whatever you want."

"Stop the gentleman act!" She pushed him gently, giggling. "I'll tell you what: you pick breakfast this time and I'll pick the breakfast next time, or lunch, depending on which comes first."

Lee liked that suggestion. "Fair enough. A fry-up it is. There's a café down this road somewhere," he guessed. "What about you? I won't feel right digging into a plate full of greased-up meat if you're sitting there swigging a cup of coffee and nibbling a slice of toast."

Zala laughed softly. "I'll join you, don't worry."

"*Really*?"

"Why do you sound so surprised?" she quizzed, her eyebrows arched.

"You don't seem like the sort of person who enjoys fried meat and eggs swimming in grease. You look more like a celery-stick-and-carrot type of person."

Zala pushed him again. "Cheeky."

"It was a compliment."

"I like my food."

"I suppose you have to, living with Riso. He must eat a lot."

Zala nodded. "He does indeed. Although he leaves very little. That's a good thing, he *hates* to waste food. If I didn't pack away those leftovers for you, he'd be forcing them down his throat right now. He hates seeing anything go to waste."

A small frumpy man in a tweed shirt walked past Lee, almost bumping into him as he passed. He shot a strange look his way, a look that suggested he hated him but couldn't remember why. Lee ignored him and continued, his attention on Zala.

"Does Riso cook you breakfast?"

"God no," Zala said sternly. "He hates cooking."

"He had fun on the barbecue last night."

"Every man has fun on a barbecue, but as soon as you put them in the kitchen, they break down."

"Good point."

"Here," Zala said quickly, holding an arm out in front of him. "What about this place?"

They were outside of a café, lined with windows and fitted with a neatly decorated sign, below which a large menu was scribbled onto a blackboard.

Lee read the menu aloud: "Bacon sandwiches, sausage sandwiches, toast, fresh juices, tea, coffee . . . " He mumbled the next few items on the list, skipping to the bottom ". . . full English breakfast." The words had been written in large letters. "Sounds good." He pushed the door open and looked into Zala's soft blue eyes. "After you?"

Seven other diners sat at three separate tables in the café. Four elderly women sat around the table closest to the door, sipping cups of coffee and chattering randomly. Lee heard the occasional *oo* and *aw* as idle conversation passed through the group like a Mexican wave. None of the women looked at Lee and Zala as they entered, content in their own little world of gossip.

Sitting at the back of the diner, as far from the ladies as possible, was an agitated man in his early twenties. He sat on the edge of his seat, his eyes constantly flickering around the café, scrutinizing each occupant many times over. His hands moved from the table—where a half-empty cup of coffee sat next to an empty breakfast plate—to his side and back again in a nervous manner. He didn't seem to know what to do with his body or his eyes, fiddling with them as if they belonged to someone else.

Between the two tables was a middle-aged couple. They sat in silence, eating bacon sandwiches and drinking cups of tea. Occasionally they looked at each other, swapping pleasant smiles and the odd comment, their words spoken in hushed whispers.

Zala and Lee sat two tables behind the silent couple, furthest away from the gossipy gathering and three tables in front of the twitchy twenty-something. Zala looked around as they sat, studying her surroundings with a look of intrigue. "This place is . . . " she paused as she looked for the right word. Her gaze crossed that of the anxious youngster, sending his nerves into rapture.

"A shit hole?" Lee offered.

Zala frowned. "*Quaint* was the word I was looking for."

"Good morning." A scruffy young waitress appeared from behind the counter. She stood next to their table, a notepad and pencil in hand. "What can I get you guys?"

"That was quick," Lee said under his breath, his eyes moving instinctively toward a rusted metal rack which propped up a menu.

"Do you want some time to look at the menu?" the waitress offered, looking like she wanted to be somewhere else and sounding like, in her head at least, she already was. Her eyes tried to cross between the pair, giving them an equal amount of contempt, but then she lingered on Lee. It was clear she had recognized him, but couldn't quite work out who he was.

"We'll have two of your full English breakfasts please," Zala said cheerfully. "With everything on." She looked at Joseph. "Is that okay?"

Joseph nodded. He'd noticed the waitress's stares and was trying to avoid her gaze, turning his attention to the tabletop, his finger idly flicking an unidentified blemish that had molded itself to the smooth plastic.

"And a pot of tea," Zala added.

Nothing was written down and nothing was said in reply. The scruffy server looked lost, staring intently at Lee's profile.

"Excuse me?" Zala said, her tone stronger and sterner.

"Hmm?" the waitress mumbled as if she had been pulled out of a trance. She managed to drag her eyes away from Lee. "Sure," she said, making a mental note of the order as she tapped the pen on the pad. "It'll be with you soon." She smiled and backed away, her eyes making detours back to Joseph's face.

Lee watched her walk around the counter. She grabbed the attention of another waitress who was busy pouring cups of tea. Words were exchanged, hushed whispers into lowered ears, and at one point both of the women looked at him. His heart banged out a few notes of annoyance and his anxiety levels increased. She had finally worked it out. The waitress knew who he was.

"I think she fancies you."

Zala's soft words broke Lee's nervous trance. He turned to face her and caught the suggestive smile on her face. He faked a laugh. "You think so?"

"Either that or she's not too smart. Only idiots, dreamers, and lovers stare, my mother used to say. And she doesn't look much like a dreamer."

"My money's on idiot."

Zala looked across at the counter. The waitress was still staring at Lee. She almost jumped when Zala met her gaze. Her eyes darted around carelessly like she didn't know where to look. "You're probably right," Zala agreed.

Moments later, the same waitress carried a tray to the table. Her appearance broke the conversation between Zala and Lee. They both leaned back in their seats, their eyes on her as she unloaded items from the plastic tray.

She slowly placed a steaming pot of tea in the center of the table, sliding empty cups before both of them. She also removed a miniature tray of assorted creams, sugar packets, and a jug of milk, placing it next to the pot. Standing up straight, she looked directly into Lee's eyes. "Your breakfast will be here shortly." She paused, pondered, and then said, "I hope you don't mind me saying, but—"

"I *do* mind," Lee quickly interrupted.

"Oh," she looked awkwardly at Zala, back at Lee, and then at her colleague behind her. She opened her mouth but words failed to form. She quickly backed away.

"She knows you?" Zala wondered.

Lee shook his head, "Maybe she was going to ask me out," he joked.

He poured tea into Zala's cup before filling his own. He noticed his hand was shaking as he reached for a packet of sugar.

"Maybe," Zala said curiously. "So, you were saying?"

"Hmm?"

"You were telling me about your work," Zala recalled.

Lee nodded, anxiously pouring two sugar packets into his cup and topping it off with a drop of milk. Looking over the shoulder of his Austrian friend, he caught the glaring eyes of one of the old ladies, who quickly averted her gaze, almost jumping out of her wrinkled skin. He was either beginning to be noticed or his paranoia was increasing. Either way, he was becoming uneasy.

"Like I said," he continued, trying to ignore the suspicion dwelling inside of him. "It's not really work."

"You live in a big house," Zala pushed. "It pays a lot of money for a hobby."

Lee smiled clumsily. "That's a different story." His eyes flickered around the café as he spoke, and he caught the stare of another old lady. She rapidly shifted her gaze.

The talk from the table of old ladies had lessened in volume. They were speaking in whispers, but whispering wasn't best performed by old, partially deaf women. The noise from their table sounded like wind rushing through open shutters. He picked up on the odd word but not enough to form a conclusion.

Zala took the hint, sensing his discomfort. "Either way," she said as she meticulously dripped milk into her tea. "You promised me you'd show me your work. Can I still hold you to that?"

"Of course, but don't get your hopes up. It's nothing special."

"Let me be the judge of that."

"Do you paint much yourself?" Lee dragged his attention away from the rest of the room, content to let his eyes rest on Zala's delicate features.

"I've tried, but I'm not very good. I prefer to observe. I never had much of a creative streak."

"But you can play the piano."

"That was all down to practice." She lifted her cup to her mouth, pursing her lips as she blew on the hot liquid. "My dad was very strict, and he insisted that I learn to play a musical instrument and learn to speak a foreign language. While the other little girls were out playing, I was inside with my piano teacher—" she took a sip from the scalding liquid and recoiled slightly as it burned her lips. "Who, incidentally, was also my English teacher."

"Talented man."

"Yes, he was. He played the piano like a true great and spoke fluent English," Zala recalled with a touch of bitterness. "He also taught me to appreciate art."

"He sounds like a good man."

"Yes. I suppose he does, doesn't he?" The bitterness was still evident.

"What about your dad?" Lee wondered. "Did he play an instrument? Was he trying to get you to follow in his footsteps or making sure you had all the things *he* didn't have?"

Zala smiled over her teacup, her curled lips cutting through the rising steam. "My teacher *was* my dad," she said wryly. "He knew a lot of things but achieved nothing. He was a good teacher but a terrible person and an even worse father."

"Oh." He hadn't been expecting that. "Sorry."

"For what?" Zala's cheeky smile had returned.

Lee shook his head. "I have no idea. It just seemed the right thing to say. Do you have any brothers or sisters?"

"Just my dad and me."

"You seem to resent him," Joseph noticed. He knew he was treading on thin ice, but Zala's expression suggested that she didn't care if he broke anything.

"Like I said, he wasn't a very good father." She locked her blue eyes into his gaze as she spoke. "I have a lot to thank him for, though. My mother died when I was three. His own parents died when he was young and he had no brothers or sisters. There was no one he could have turned to for help. He raised me on his own."

"He did a brilliant job. You've turned out perfectly fine."

"Thank you."

"Although I've only known you for a day, you could have a closet full of skeletons."

She shook her head, grinned slyly. "I don't keep them in the closet."

Lee smiled. "So, why the hatred for your father then?" he enquired, adding the obligatory, "If you don't mind me asking."

"He had a somewhat *alternative* view to parenting. I was more his pupil than his daughter. He beat me when I did wrong. He had a set of rules and a belt for every rule that I broke. He was very organized that way." She paused to drink; Lee was too shocked to interject.

"He didn't really take me anywhere or even embrace me. I can't remember him telling me he loved me, ever." Zala noticed the shock in Lee's eyes. "Don't look so startled. That was years ago and my childhood wasn't a total failure. He did teach me what he knew and if it hadn't have been for his teachings, God knows where I would be today. In the small town where I grew up, hardly any of the children went to school. If it wasn't for my father and his strict ways, I would have never had an education and I probably wouldn't have met Riso."

Lee sighed, not sure how to reply. He had his own problems and his own troubled past that he couldn't talk about, and dealing with someone else's was alien to him. "Why didn't your father put any of his own abilities to good use?"

"The short answer?" Zala sighed softly. "He was a drunken coward who liked to gamble too much."

"And the long answer . . . dare I ask?"

Warmth emanated from Zala's smile. She seemed comfortable talking to Lee about her past and he was more than happy to listen.

"He was a talented, educated man. In his youth, he taught himself many things. He learned to appreciate art; he studied music and became a skilled pianist and violinist. He also studied literature, history, and philosophy. He served in the army and traveled the world, developing a love of culture and language. In his twenties, he met and fell in love with my mother. He left the army and took on several low-paying jobs, hoping, one day to move to England, start a family, and begin a new life. He adored England."

Lee nodded. "So what happened?"

"*I did,*" Zala said, taking another drink of tea. "I wasn't planned, I came too early. My birth set his plans back a few years." She sighed again, a sigh of remembrance and sympathy for the family she'd lost and the dreams that had gone with them. "Then my mother died and my dad . . . well, he 'lost the plot', as you say."

"Ah," Lee understood more than Zala knew. He too had "lost the plot" after the death of his wife.

"After her death, he lost interest in doing all the things he'd dreamed of, and, instead, he pushed all of his lost dreams onto me."

"You *have* achieved his dreams, though, right?"

"Yes, I suppose I have." She smiled contently, pausing momentarily, "You know, you're really easy to talk to. There's something so sweet and attentive behind those dark eyes."

Lee stared deeply into Zala's eyes. Their penetrating gazes were quickly broken by the sight of two large plates, filled to the brim with greased meat, black pudding, beans, toast, eggs, tomatoes, and mushrooms. Their breakfast had arrived.

The two heart-clogging meals were plonked onto the table by the disheveled waitress, the grease wobbling from the vibration. "There you go," she spoke blankly over the sound of ceramic shuddering against the plastic table top. "Enjoy." Her words lacked sincerity, and she turned and left as soon as they were spoken.

Lee watched her leave, a look of disbelief etched across his face. "Charming little fucker, isn't she?"

8

Joseph Lee finished his breakfast with delight. He would have licked the plate if he was alone. The conversation had flowed, almost between bites. They both seemed to take great pleasure in listening to what the other had to say, no matter how trivial.

Her appetite wasn't as great as his. She left a rasher of bacon, a half-eaten sausage, both of her slices of black pudding—she'd seen it being made as a teenager and wanted no part in eating it—and a scoop of beans and tomatoes. She was a slow eater, still nibbling on her last piece of toast after Lee had cleared his plate.

"You certainly *were* hungry," she noted, gesturing to his empty plate. "Do you want anything else or should we get going?"

Lee looked around. The twitchy twenty-year-old had hastily left earlier, followed by the silent couple, who had left with a touch of serenity—their faces alight, their arms interlocked. The old ladies remained and had been talking in whispers throughout, their coffee cups constantly being filled by the unkempt, ill-mannered waitress who, on several occasions, had joined in with their hushed chatter. Lee knew they were talking about him, their idle conversation moving on from wondering if he was the man whose wife had been brutally murdered to gossiping about how he'd gone mad, savagely killed her, stole her inheritance, and then miraculously freed himself from the long arm of the law.

He had heard it all before but he no longer cared. Zala attracted all of his attention and forced his anxieties away.

"I'm stuffed. Let's get out of here." He stood, reached for his wallet, and walked up to the counter where both waitresses waited for him.

"Hey!" Zala objected. "*I* invited *you*, I should pay."

"No chance." Lee shook off the comment. "You fed me last night; it's only fair I feed you this morning."

She shrugged in reluctant agreement and walked by his side. Lee studied one of the many menus on the counter. He calculated the cost of the breakfast in his head, not too keen on starting a conversation with either of the sour-faced waitresses. He took out the exact change, laid it on the counter, and pushed it toward the glaring inquisitors. "There you go," he said without making eye contact.

"Wait!" the bland waitress called as Lee turned to leave. "Can I ask you something?"

He didn't turn around.

As they passed the group of old ladies, Lee noted that each one of them stopped chatting and simultaneously turned to look at him. One of them twisted almost supernaturally on her chair. Threats hung in their stares: *We know who you are, You murderous bastard, You insane weirdo,* but none of them said a word. They had conspired with the waitress in a plot to intimidate the innocent man, but they weren't counting on him speaking.

"What?" Lee spat, stopping in front of the woman who had twisted her body awkwardly just to glare at him. "What do you want?"

One of them mumbled incoherently; another turned away; the twisted woman looked down at the floor, her twist now a yoga pose.

Lee raised his eyebrows at the fourth woman who had yet to react. "I know who you are," she said, as though her words were going to send Joseph into a rhapsody of tears and regret.

Lee turned to Zala. "It seems I'm a local celebrity," he said calmly with a feigned touch of pride. He shook away his anger, told himself they weren't worth it, and then moved to escort Zala out of the diner.

They weren't going to let him walk free though, and one of the old ladies shouted after him as he reached the door: "We all know what you *did*."

Lee paused again. "I'm sorry, Zala, can you please wait outside?" He glanced back at the nagging women. "I'll explain all of this to you later. I promise."

Zala did as was instructed and calmly left the café. Lee walked back to the table, pulled up a chair, and made himself comfortable. "What exactly did I do?" he asked politely.

The women looked shocked at first, almost horrified. The one furthest away from him, feeling safer, spoke first. "You killed your wife," she accused.

"Then you ran away," another chimed as the confidence of the group grew.

Lee laughed. "Did I now." He spoke bitterly through gritted teeth; he could feel the frustration and anger growing inside of him. "I didn't kill my wife. Killers go to jail. As much of a shit hole as this is, it's certainly not jail and I didn't run away. If you want to criticize and speculate, I suggest you pick up a newspaper now and then. It may not be entirely accurate, but it's better than getting all your information from gossiping, illiterate, senile old fucks."

"Hey!" the two waitresses had moved from behind the counter and were advancing on the table. "We don't tolerate that kind of language in here," one of them warned.

"And we don't want your kind here either," the other added.

Lee shook his head in disbelief and stood with deliberate haste. All the women at the table flinched, a startled noise—the last gasp of a trampled rodent—escaping from their lips. The waitresses took a step backward.

Lee merely smiled, grinning at each of them in turn. He returned the chair to the empty table and left the building.

"What was all that about?" Zala was standing outside, leaning against the wall of the café, her expression surprisingly relaxed.

Lee sighed. He didn't want Zala to know about Jennifer, lest she judge him just like everyone else. He motioned for her to walk with him down the street. "There are a few things I haven't told you . . . " he began as they strode away from the diner.

He had only known her for a day, and he reasoned that she didn't know him enough to trust him. She didn't know him enough to believe he was innocent. But, unlike the gossiping old townspeople, Zala had intelligence and an open mind. She had also told him about her own troubled past, so she did trust him to an extent.

"But now isn't the time," he continued. "I'll tell you later, when we're less . . . " He looked around at the swarms of people on the street. "Surrounded," he finished uncomfortably.

"Oh, okay."

"I'm sorry for losing it in there," he apologized. "I'm not normally like that, I don't have a short fuse I just . . . "

"You're a nice man," Zala finished for him. "I'm sure you have good reason. You can invite me over for a coffee when we get back home and you can explain yourself then."

Joseph opened his mouth to speak but realized that Zala had done all the talking for him. He smiled. "Fair enough."

9

As afternoon broke, Zala Lechnen and Joseph Lee made their way home, taking a more direct route. Zala was a talkative woman, and she had a lot to say. But behind the wheel, her concentration levels increased and her desire for conversation decreased.

Joseph had shown her around town, winging it all the way. It had changed a lot since he had last been. They visited a picturesque sweet shop at the bottom of the street. The exterior was alight with fancy signs and colorful artwork; jars of brightly colored sweets gleamed through the windows. A little old woman owned the shop and was the only one inside. Luckily for Lee, she didn't seem to recognize him, allowing for a tension-free stroll around the shop as Zala studied the shelves of confectionary with the delight of a child.

"We're the only sweet shop in town," the chatty shop owner had declared proudly. "And we've been in business for more than sixty years now. My dad owned the shop before me and my son will own it after me."

They left the shop with an assortment of boiled sweets, all wrapped in separate paper bags, including a large bag of chocolate-covered raisins and peanuts that Zala had bought for Riso. Lee bought nothing. The sickly-sweet smell in the shop, layered on top of the greasy breakfast in his stomach, was almost enough to make him sick.

At a newsstand, Zala bought both a national and a local newspaper and signed up to receive regular deliveries of both. She also stocked up on milk and bread from an adjacent co-op, buying herself and Lee a bottle of pop, which they drank as they walked through the streets.

She stuck to her word and didn't drag Lee into any clothing shops, although she did plenty of window-shopping. Lee insisted that he didn't mind if she looked around, but she brushed off his comments. She also bought some DVDs from a charity shop, and after mocking her for bypassing the digital revolution, Lee happily agreed to watch one of them with her. They chose together, picking a copy of a classic horror title to go along with an old James Bond release—apparently Riso was a huge fan, which didn't come as much of a surprise to Joseph.

They spoke constantly but never about what happened in the café. Despite his anxiety about being outside, among what his paranoia told him was a crowd of people who all thought he was a murderer, Lee thoroughly enjoyed himself. He was so consumed with Zala that he hadn't deluded himself with what others might have been thinking or saying behind his back.

They finished off the morning with a drink and a game of pool at one of the local pubs. Zala ordered a small glass of lemonade while Lee chugged two pints of lager. Her slow, steady, and haphazard style of play triumphed. She beat him seven games to five, teasing him all the way back to the car.

Joseph looked across at her. He waited until she nervously reversed out of the car park before he spoke. "You're not a very confident driver are you?"

Zala merely laughed.

"How long have you been driving?"

"Only a year."

"You should have told me that before," he spoke quickly, feigning anxiety as he glanced out of the side window. "I wouldn't have gotten in the car with you if I'd known."

"Cheeky!"

"How—" the sound of a mobile phone interrupted him.

Zala shifted uncomfortably. "Damn," she muttered. "Can you get that? It's probably just Riso. Here—" She gestured toward her jacket pocket with a thrust of her hips. "If you don't mind."

Without hesitation, Joseph dug his hand into the pocket and retrieved a large black smartphone. The face was alight with an orange glow, the words *my darling riso* superimposed over the orange background. He struggled to work the device. He hadn't used a mobile phone for years. It felt so brittle in his hands, so delicate and responsive to his callous touch.

"Drag the bar across," Zala instructed.

He managed to answer the call. He stared at the phone unsurely for a few moments, dragging it to his ear when he heard an expectant voice crackle out of it.

"Hello?"

"Hey!" Riso hesitated momentarily. "Mr. Lee?"

"Yes," Lee confirmed, suddenly aware that he was nodding. He quickly stopped. "Zala is driving."

"Ah I see. So she hasn't killed you yet then!"

Lee laughed awkwardly.

"She's a funny thing behind the wheel. Is she sticking out her tongue?"

Lee looked across at the concentrated driver. "Yes."

"Has she blinked yet?"

He laughed again. "Just once or twice."

Riso's coarse laugh echoed venomously down the line. Lee found himself pulling the device away from his ear.

"How have you two been today?" the big Austrian enquired. "She's been treating you okay, I hope?"

"Yes, it's been fun." He felt slightly awkward about telling a husband how much fun he'd had with his wife.

"I'm glad you two enjoyed yourself." He seemed genuinely happy. "I just phoned to tell her I'll be home late tonight. This place is falling apart without me, work is piling up."

"Okay."

"Tell her not to bother cooking me anything. I'll grab a big greasy takeaway on my way home. It beats home-cooking any day, if you ask me."

Lee laughed.

"Don't tell her I said that, though."

"Of course."

"Tell her I'll phone her later, would you?"

"I will do."

"I'll speak to you soon. Don't be a stranger, right?"

"I won't. See you later, Riso." He lowered the phone, waited to make sure the call had ended, and then slipped it back into Zala's pocket.

"What did he have to say?" she wondered. They were less than a minute from home. Lee was very impressed and some-what amazed at her sense of direction. She hadn't once asked him which turning to take.

"He's busy at work. He says he won't be back until late and not to bother cooking him anything." He kindly left out the part about the takeaway. "He said he'll call you later."

Zala sighed. "Ah well," she said, her eyes never leaving the road. "Are *you* busy tonight?"

"Me? No."

"How about we order a pizza, grab a few beers, and watch that film?"

A smile spread from ear to ear. "I'd love to."

"You can also explain the café incident," she added.

The smile flickered but remained. "Sure."

10

Joseph Lee settled in front of the television and stared at the clock above it. It was five minutes to seven. He watched the minute hand tick over in anticipation and wondered about the night ahead and the day that preceded it.

After his artery-clogging breakfast, his insatiable appetite had remained. He reheated some of the leftover meat, opened a can of beans, and combined the two. Zala had retired to her house and would arrive at seven.

Lee hadn't welcomed guests in a long time. In fact, *he* had *never* welcomed guests. Jennifer had the social life; she had been the entertainer, not him. There had been numerous occasions when guests had been in the house and Lee had hidden away upstairs, preferring to sit and paint than engage in conversation.

After finishing his meal, he rushed around the house with an obsessive-compulsive flair. He removed empty bottles and cans from the floors and washed away visible grime, grease, and dirt. He washed the bathroom floors, scrubbed the kitchen floor, and ran a vacuum cleaner over the carpets.

Armed with a spray bottle and a cloth, he washed down the window sills, the kitchen cupboards, tables, chairs, television. And he removed the splashes of dirt from the living room walls.

He didn't want the house to look like it had been inhabited by a depressed hermit for a year, even if it had been.

He thought about cleaning the sofa but wasn't entirely sure how. He guessed he could figure out how to remove the covers from the cushions but doubted he could figure out how to wash them, dry them, and replace them in time. Instead he sprayed them, practically soaking them, with Febreze and flipped them over, stain-side down.

He finished at six, out of breath, red-faced and exhausted. After cleaning the house, he went to work on himself—a shorter, easier task. He showered, changed into a clean pair of clothes, and relaxed on the bed for a while, waiting for his heart to slow and for two painkillers to kick in and rid him of a nasty headache.

The housework had driven all the energy out of him. To force some back in, he dropped a couple of caffeine pills and washed them down with an energy drink, both of which he used regularly to keep himself awake on the nights he refused to dream.

He was relaxed and calm.

He flicked on the television and lowered the volume.

He watched the minute hand drop another notch.

Along with the smell of Febreze, which purged from the sofa, his senses flared with a fresh meadow scent. He had covered the house with air freshener, removing the stale lived-in smell. His mind had been running riot with thoughts of what the Austrian would think. What would she think of his house, what would she think of *him*? He was nervous and tense. He felt like he was back in college trying to impress a fellow student—although the only fellow student he had ever tried to impress was Jennifer.

The sound of knocking interrupted his thoughts. She was on time. He rushed to the door, stopping to check his appearance before preparing a welcoming smile.

Zala Lechnen glowed. She wore blue jeans that opened slightly around her lower thighs and legs, giving a baggy appearance, but clinging tightly to her buttocks and tops of her thighs. She wore a frilly white shawl, wide and short. It spread across her chest like a sheet, covering her breasts and draping loosely from her delicate shoulders. The material stopped just above her navel, revealing her flat, tanned stomach.

A beautiful glow radiated from her face. Her soft skin was illuminated by a fine layer of foundation; her bright blue eyes lit by a soft strip of eyeliner and framed with deep black mascara. Her hair remained the same, but looked a touch curlier and seemed to shine in the glow of the streetlights.

She held the DVD and a plastic bag that bulged promisingly with cans of lager. Lee stepped aside, inhaling her sensual scent as she shuffled past.

She walked straight into the living room in her usual relaxed and forward manner. Her eyes scanned her surroundings. "I'm impressed," she said, nodding in approval.

"With what?" Lee closed the door and followed her as she made her way around the room.

"With the house. For a single man, you've managed to keep the place in good condition. I was half expecting piles of pizza boxes and empty cans of lager. I thought I would have to swim in."

Lee smirked guiltily. "Thanks." He stared at the arch of her back and traced the curve of her spine until his eyes rested on her buttocks. He immediately pulled his gaze away, worried she would catch him.

"Let me take those." He reached for the bag in her hand. She allowed him to take it, her eyes still surveying the freshly cleaned interior.

He took it to the kitchen and began to remove the cans, placing them in the fridge. "Thanks for bringing the booze," he shouted, his head buried in the fridge. "I normally have a fridge full of lager but I haven't been shopping recently. I'm short a few things." As he looked into the bare fridge, he almost laughed at the understatement.

"No problem," Zala called. "I need to do some shopping myself. Riso goes through food like you wouldn't believe."

Lee had seen the man eat—he *could* believe it.

"How do you get your groceries in if you don't have a car?" she wondered. "The closest supermarket is a twenty-minute drive away, isn't it?"

"I do it online; it's a lot easier and saves a lot of hassle."

Zala mumbled an agreement from the next room. "Have you just painted?" she wondered.

He finished stacking the cans in the fridge, left two on the countertop. "No, why?" He ripped open the cans, pouring the frothy liquid into two glasses.

"Your walls seem a little bare."

"What were you expecting?"

"You're an artist . . . " she pondered. "I was expecting *art*."

"I'm not a big art lover. I appreciate it but not enough to pin it to my walls or stand and admire it." He crunched up an empty can and tossed it toward the bin; it bounced off the metallic rim and clattered to the floor.

"What about your own art?"

"I like that even less; it depresses me. If I stare at it long enough, I start to question myself, *why did I paint this, why didn't I paint that, I should have done this, I should have done that*." He finished pouring the second can. The empty aluminium tin landed successfully in the bin this time. "Plus, it seems a bit pretentious to cover your house in your own work."

Zala disagreed. "It shows that you have pride in what you do. Your home is a reflection of yourself, so what better way to reflect that part of yourself than by filling it with images of your own imagination and works of your own creation?"

"I suppose." He picked up the fallen can from the floor and dropped it into the bin, using his socks to wipe up the spillage.

He took the two pints and walked back into the living room, handing one of them to his appreciative guest.

"Cheers," they said simultaneously, touching glasses.

Zala handed Lee the DVD and then cautiously sat down on the sofa, careful not to spill the brimming beer over the edge of the glass.

"What about pictures?"

"Hmm?" Lee mumbled, opening the tray for the DVD player and flicking on the television.

"Photographs, portraits, family pictures; pictures of you in your youth. There's nothing." She raised the glass to her lips and then quickly withdrew it. "Sorry if I'm asking too many questions. Just tell me to shut up if I'm annoying you."

Lee laughed noiselessly. "I wouldn't dream of it." He straightened up. The DVD loaded in the player, whirring noisily. The television screen turned from blue to black. "I don't know really. I guess I'm just not very sentimental."

He didn't want to tell her the truth—that he had hidden all his paintings for the benefit of his own sanity. She would ask about Jennifer and he would tell her. He'd promised to. But he wanted to have a few drinks first.

"I am a man, after all."

Zala chuckled. "Good point."

———

The movie finished with a flurry of gore and screams. Lee found himself cringing as blood splattered and limbs dismembered. Zala didn't flinch. She watched the entire film with a smile on her face. He didn't see a hint of sadism in her eyes, though, just contentment. The pause button had been pressed several times, their glasses filled with beer on each occasion. They drank four pints in two hours, finishing their fifth just as the screen faded to black and the credits rolled.

"That was fun," Zala said excitedly, her speech slightly slurred.

"Yep. Want another?" Lee motioned to her glass, a small amount of foamy liquid in the bottom.

Zala nodded. She drained the glass and handed it to Lee, sighing pleasantly. As he made his way to the kitchen, she leaned back on the sofa, stretching her arms above her head and yawning pleasurably, finishing with a loud groan. She stretched her legs, resting her hands on her thighs as she brought her feet parallel to her knees and flexed her toes.

Lee watched her lustfully from the kitchen, her view of him obscured. He refilled the glasses, noting that only two cans remained in the fridge and cursing at himself for not stocking up. When he returned to the sofa, Zala was staring at him—her body slouched, her head sunk into the cushions. She looked relaxed, almost sedated. She grinned widely as she took the glass from him, holding it steady above her lap.

"So tell me, Mr. Lee," she said placidly, her voice delicate. "What exactly is it you do? I think I'm due an explanation, am I not?" she carefully dragged her body upright.

Lee rested back and turned his head to face her. "It's a long story."

"Shorten it."

"Well, technically I don't do anything. I don't work, and to be honest, I never really have. I'm what you might call a professional slouch."

"Go on."

"The money, the house," he paused, "everything really, is, *was,* my wife's." He stopped, finding the memories difficult to recall.

"You have a troubled past," she noted, hoping to comfort him. "We have that in common. If you don't want to talk about it, that's okay, I don't want to make things awkward for you."

Lee shook his head. "I want to talk about it, it's just not very easy." He feigned a laugh.

She offered him a starting point. "What was your wife's name?"

"Jennifer." He smiled at her memory, looking across at Zala. "She looked a lot like you. The same eyes, the same smile; she was an amazing woman." He retracted his gaze awkwardly.

"You have mentioned her name a few times," Zala said warmly. "You said her name the first time you saw me. I've been wondering about that. I suppose it makes sense now. So . . . what was she like, what did she do?"

"She was amazing, generous, sweet. She had a lot of time for me when no one else did. When we met, I was a social outcast, my relationships lasted days and normally ended in feuds. My friendships lasted longer but ended in fights. I was always a loner, but I liked it that way. You could say I was independent and free but it was more like unsociable and hate-filled. Jennifer changed that. She became my best friend and my lover; she even helped recoup my relationships with my family, who I'd pushed out of my life." Lee looked away from Zala as he spoke, staring at the television as if the blank screen helped his recall.

"She was a career-driven woman, she loved her work," he concluded.

"What did she do?"

"She was a lawyer, a very successful one. She bought this house. Her parents left her a fortune in their will but I don't think she touched a penny. She didn't need to." He took a sip of his beer, grimaced at the memory of his in-laws. "They hated me, all of her family did."

"Why?"

"Because I was a nobody. I still am. I never worked. I never held down a job. They were all successful, hardworking people so they resented me. They said I was leeching off Jennifer, using her for her money. A set of fucking wankers, if you ask me. I never paid attention to them anyway. Her dad was a stuck-up prick who spent his days playing golf and drinking; her mother was hooked on more prescription meds than Elvis."

"You shouldn't have taken their judgements to heart. They don't seem like decent people themselves. Who are they to judge?"

"I didn't really care what they thought." He sighed and sank back into the sofa, falling silent.

"What about your family?" Zala wondered.

"They're good people. Not as well-off but not as judgemental either." He took a deep breath and met Zala's caring gaze. "My wife was murdered nearly a year ago," he said abruptly.

Zala's eyes widened, shocked, but she didn't move or avert her gaze. "I'm sorry to hear that." She sounded genuine.

"I was the prime suspect," Joseph explained. "They were sure I killed her, neglecting the fact that I was unconscious and bleeding at the time. My face was plastered all over the news. The story covered the entire district, every local paper and TV station had me pinned as the murderer. I was never officially arrested or charged, but the motive was enough to convict me in the eyes of the press." He looked deeply into Zala's eyes. She was following every word. "I didn't kill her; I would never have done such a thing."

Zala nodded.

"The whole town turned against me, even my own family broke off contact. My brother and sister-in-law were supposed to come around on the night of Jennifer's murder. They arrived an hour after the police. They were treated as suspects as well and they resented *me* for it. They thought I was guilty. I haven't seen them since."

"If the police believed you then why didn't everyone else?"

"The press had the power, not the police. They tried to arrest me, they tried their best, but they gave up. They had to.

The press never gave up; news is news, and news about Jennifer sold well. People don't tend to listen to the boring truth when someone else is spreading interesting lies." He took a drink, drained half of the liquid in the glass. "I got into some trouble as a teenager," he explained to Zala's open and sympathetic ears, "Quite a few times actually. I rounded it all off by assaulting a man twice my age. They said I was deluded and paranoid, that I had a lot of anger issues."

"Did you?"

"Definitely. I was a mess. I spent three years on medication, and for the first six months, they dumped me in a psychiatric hospital."

"You seem perfectly fine to me."

"I am *now*," he confirmed. "I got my life back on track, promised the mental health team I would start a college course, which I did. Not long after that, I met Jennifer and the rest was history. She sorted me out. But my history, along with the motive of all Jennifer's money, was enough to fill the front pages. I inherited everything she owned, which, by default, was also everything her parents owned. She fixed me in life and looked after me in death."

"I see," Zala said, clearly unsure how to respond.

"I turned back into a social misfit when she died. Last night and then today was the first time I've left the house in months. I found it so hard to continue without her . . . " He finished the rest of his drink and retired from the room into the kitchen.

Zala knew about Jennifer and he felt uncomfortable about that. He couldn't explain any further. He crumpled over the kitchen counter, resting his palms on the marbled surface and sinking his head into his chest. He expected her to leave, maybe out of fear, maybe out of mistrust.

"Are you okay?" She stood behind him, her hand hovering gently over his shoulder, ready to comfort him but not sure if he wanted to be comforted.

She allowed her hand to rest on his shoulder, his muscles twitched. She held her palm in place.

"It took a lot of courage for you to tell me that." Her voice was soft and comforting.

He straightened up and turned to face her. "I didn't kill her."

Zala nodded. "I believe you, and so did the police, that makes you innocent in my book."

"You can leave if you feel uncomfortable," he said.

Zala rubbed her chin. "Hmm," she pondered lightly. "I have a better idea." She produced her mobile phone from her pocket. "Why don't we stop this depressive talk, order a pizza, and watch some television?"

He laughed, agreed. "Cheers," he said softly.

"For what? Go and sit down, you big softy. Find the number for the pizza place. I'm starving!"

They returned to the sofa and found a talk show, which they watched with the volume lowered. They drank the final two beers, both of them merry, tipsy, and relaxed. The conversation stayed light and unobtrusive, and Lee's mood gradually increased until he felt comfortable in his own skin again. Only then did he return to the conversation.

"Doesn't it make you uncomfortable?" he wondered.

"Hmm?"

Lee noticed that the carefree expression had remained on Zala's face, only faltering when he recalled the murderous events of the previous year. "Now that you know that my wife was murdered."

"Not really. I feel bad for you. *That* makes me uncomfortable. Other than that, no, unless . . . " Her eyes quickly darted around the house. "She's not haunting the place, is she?"

Lee laughed. "No."

"Then no," Zala confirmed with a grin. "Sorry to joke about it like that. Laughter is the best medicine as they say, and over the years I've learned that making light of life's painful moments is the best way to get through them."

"You're probably right."

"It was a bit of a surprise, though, I have to admit," she confessed. "I knew you were hiding some painful memories, and at first I thought it may have been a bad divorce—"

"It was," Lee interjected light-heartedly.

She pushed him gently before continuing, "But what happened in the café swayed my thoughts a bit."

"Jennifer had a lot of friends and none of them liked me. Most of them didn't even know me. They turned against me when she died. They blamed me. What appeared in the news, the motives and what not, just fueled their hatred. The old gits in the café were probably friends of friends."

"Or maybe just gossiping old biddies with nothing better to do?"

"Possibly."

"Well, Mr. Lee," she said with a deep breath, simulating seriousness before smiling and breaking it. "I'm on your side from now on."

———

The pizza arrived half an hour later. They turned off the television and the show they hadn't really been watching and sat on the sofa with pizza boxes in their laps.

"I don't know how you can eat that." Zala finished off a mouthful of pepperoni and gestured toward the open box on Lee's lap.

"You ever tried it?" he asked, tucking into the thick layers of cheese, dotted with ham and pineapple.

"Yes, it's . . . " she looked for the right word, nibbling on a bit of crust. She had an unusual way of eating the pizza. She nibbled away the crusts first then rotated the slice and ate from the point. "Unusual," she finished.

"I *am* unusual."

"I agree," she said with a mouthful of food. "But pineapple on a pizza? That's too much. It's beyond unusual, stretching into the boundaries of absurd. Show me the guy who first put fruit on a pizza, and I'll show you a raging homosexual with a fetish for Hawaiian shirts."

"He sounds like a nice guy."

"Have you ever had cherries or banana on a pizza?" Zala wondered.

"No."

"Would you?"

"No."

"Why?"

"Because that's just weird."

"Exactly. Fruit does not belong on a pizza."

"Isn't tomato a fruit?"

"I don't think so."

"I'm sure it is. It's one of those fruits that everyone thinks is a vegetable."

"You're thinking of something else," Zala assured. "Strawberries probably." She laughed, firing bread shrapnel over the floor.

Lee laughed as well, his cheeks bulging like a hamster.

"I've eaten like a pig today," she said lightly as she began to deprive another slice of its crust. "Riso would be proud. I'll have to work it off in the gym."

"Have you joined a gym around here?" Lee's attention moved from his pizza to Zala.

"I have some equipment at home." She paused to swallow. "Well, I have an exercise bike. Are there any good gyms nearby?"

"You're asking the wrong man. Surely Riso goes to the gym?"

"He *did*. He hasn't found one up here yet. He goes to different gyms though, less machines, more weights." She spoke between chews. "He says a gym shouldn't be populated by middle-aged women sweating on treadmills or hyperventilating on rowing machines. He prefers the free weights, barbell-only type places. Full of testosterone-pumped bodybuilders. I'd be careful if I were you, he might try to drag you into one. He'll be looking for a training partner."

"What's that supposed to mean? I can handle myself."

Zala laughed at the comment. She held her hand to her mouth to stop the food from shooting out.

"I used to workout quite a bit," Lee said in defense. "It's been awhile, to be fair . . . "

"You should get back into it, shed some of that puppy fat." She tapped a hand on his midsection, beating out a hollow drumming sound from the roll of fat that hung around his lazy waist.

Lee imagined his current physical state being put through its paces in the gym. "Maybe I'll just think of an excuse if Riso asks me to go with him."

"Make it a good one, he can be convincing."

"Anyone his size can be convincing."

"Oh," she barked, a memory jumping into her head. "That reminds me: I think he wants to dig the garden up. He likes to keep up appearances and says the garden looks unkempt. He might ask you to help him out this weekend, do some male bonding."

Lee nodded. "I need to sort mine out, as well. It's wild out there. More weeds than flowers—more weeds than *grass*."

"He'll help you out. It should be nice this weekend. I might even join you guys." Zala was down to her last piece of pizza, which she had singled out for special treatment. She was saving the crust for last.

"There'll be a lot of digging," Lee said, remembering the mass of weeds and overgrown foliage that had amassed in both of their gardens, especially his. "You won't need to go to a gym if you help us out."

"I'll supervise. I hate getting dirty."

Lee finished his pizza and washed it down with what remained of his beer. Zala soon followed. She then rested back on the sofa, holding her stomach and sighing softly.

"I'm stuffed," she said, her eyes half closed. "I'll have to get going soon, Riso will be home." She raised her hand to her mouth to cover an inaudible burp, which she politely apologized for. "I hope he isn't hungry. I can't be bothered to make him anything."

"It's nearly ten," Lee noted. "It's too late to cook. If he's hungry he won't want much, surely. He can wait until morning."

Zala shook her head lazily. "Not Riso. He's like a baby. If he isn't fed, he probably won't sleep. I'll be up with him all night."

"I suppose a man like him needs to eat."

"A man like him never *stops* eating."

Within minutes, Lee watched Zala quickly deteriorate, her eyes heavier, her words slower, slurred and more incoherent. They watched television in silence, until Lee also felt a swarm of tiredness creep over him.

Before they both fell asleep on the sofa, she wished him a goodnight with a soft yawn and a gentle kiss on the cheek. Joseph watched her stumble across the road and disappear into her house. He smiled deeply to himself, knowing he was in for a rare good night's sleep.

11

The next few days passed quickly and smoothly, steeped in a contentment that had previously been banished from Joseph Lee's life. He no longer felt the need to plug his days with monotonous activities and mundane tasks to pass time and skip from tedious minute to tedious minute. In the mornings, he woke with a smile and not a start. His dreams were obscure, meaningless and light. The images of Jennifer's slaughtered corpse no longer entered his sleeping mind, nor did they find their way into his vegetated waking state.

He didn't stare meaninglessly anymore and didn't force his mind from reality. Everything he did, every activity he engaged in, was no longer overshadowed by boredom and feelings of pointlessness. He began to enjoy things again, engaging with the world.

He also found the creativity to paint and write again. A flood of inspiration entered his mind, expanding throughout the hollow void. He wrote sonnets and odes to his own depression, allowing his previous feelings of hopelessness to fill out the pages. He also wrote limericks and comical couplets while drunk and merry one night. He painted pictures of the view beyond the tall windows, the street, the gardens, the opposing houses. He drew inspiration from pictures and magazine covers, even sketching a portrait of a soap star he found on the front of a magazine that had dropped through his door.

He painted Zala Lechnen, changing her appearance with shades and marks that linked more to her warm personality than her striking beauty, ensuring memories of Jennifer stayed away. One morning, as he looked out of the expansive studio windows with the sun beaming a bright orange glow over the street, he watched Zala sunbathing on her front lawn, taking in as much of the autumn sunshine as she could. He painted her as she lay, surrounded by the leafy garden and the backdrop of the house. She was the centerpiece of the painting, her golden skin glowing, her glossy hair glittering, her slender body relaxed and reclined.

He hung that painting and a few others on the walls of the studio, bringing color back into the bright room. He also rehung some of his favorite artwork to help decorate the walls, making sure that Jennifer appeared in none of them. The beautiful Austrian—who had inspired his sudden change of mood— had been to see him every day. She came to his house for coffee and chit-chats and he repaid the gesture. They shared mindless banter and swapped opinions on everything from pop music to politics. They had a lot of interests in common, and what they didn't have in common they teased each other about.

Lee also spent time with Riso, seeing the giant after work and enjoying the odd beer with him. He also spent another night at the Lechnens' house after being invited over for dinner. While sharing another hefty meal, he dug deeper into the big man's past and shared some of his own. The more time he spent with Riso, the more he liked him. Despite their growing friendship, Riso still didn't know about Jennifer. Zala decided against telling her husband about their conversation, insisting personal information that affected someone's past and psyche as much as Jennifer's death had was something not to be shared. If Riso was to know, it would have to come from Lee's mouth, but he hadn't said a word. He wasn't ashamed or scared of what the man might think—he seemed just as caring and compassionate as Zala—but something else swayed him.

It was easy to talk to Zala about it. She was warm and inviting and had also told Lee about her own past. But something told Lee that the same talk with Riso would somehow push them further away, turning their friendship into an uncomfortable one.

The day after their chat, Zala had taken Lee to the supermarket to stock up. Lee kept his load light, buying only bare necessities. Zala shopped like a woman possessed, buying masses of meat, protein-rich processed dinners, and the odd sugary treat for a husband with a ravenous appetite. With each passing day, each visit, and each trip, Lee's mood lifted further. The lighter mood was also a boost to his personal hygiene. He now showered and changed into fresh clothes daily. He no longer slept on the couch soaked in his own bodily fluids. He cleaned the house regularly and even began to eat normally.

His mood lifted sporadically every time he received a smile or cheeky grin from Zala. He adored her and she warmed his heart—half of him wanted her and lusted after her, the other half refused to get emotionally involved with a married woman and destroy two friendships that had helped him so much. He was in a happy limbo where he could enjoy her company and her friendship. Anything else could damage that, or break up a marriage and drag Lee back into a relationship that he wasn't ready for.

One Friday night over dinner, Lee and Riso decided that they would work on both of their gardens over the weekend. Riso had the weekend off from work and the state of the garden had been bugging him. Lee wanted to spend more time with his new friends. To ready the ground for next season, they would literally tear it apart; strip it of all the dying flowers, booming weeds, and dead grass and then let the weather do its work for a few months.

When Joseph Lee woke on the Saturday morning, he woke with a smile on his face and memories of a beautiful dream still fresh in his mind. He had dreamed he was flying over the top of his house, circling around it. Spinning and twisting in the air, he edged his way away from his house and hovered over the garden of the Lechnens' house, pushing through the wind like a swimmer through water.

He landed on the ground, his body falling effortlessly into a sun lounger. He began to speak. He wasn't sure who he was speaking to and doubted if anyone was there, but in the dream it felt normal. It felt good. He spoke for several minutes, relaying his deepest emotions and most twisted depressions with a sense of serenity, the smile constant on his content face. He then moved again.

He was in a car, watching the world pass by. He watched people in their gardens, lighting barbecues and exchanging conversation. He noted distant fields filled with human-ants playing football or rugby and he studied the exterior of many shops and restaurants, all filled to the brim. All the while he was still speaking, telling someone of his fears, relating personal things about himself he was sure he would never tell another human being.

He awoke during the car journey, a sense of delight still warming him. He wondered about the dream, and he immediately contemplated his words and who they were spoken to. Zala was the first suspect to jump into his mind but his dreaming state had made no announcement of her presence, even as he floated over her house, he hadn't recalled seeing her or thinking about her. He had been the only person in the dream, the others mere passing scenery that only existed for his amusement. He was the only person in the world yet he was merely a spectator.

Clearing his throat of a dry tingle, he shrugged off the dream and lifted his legs out of bed, swinging his body after them. He didn't care what the dream was about. It made him feel good, and that's what mattered. There was no better way to start the day.

He showered with the radio on, singing along to the songs even though he was hearing them for the first time. He climbed out of the shower, danced naked in front of the mirror, laughing at himself as he shaved. He ran down the stairs, jumped and slid across the laminated hallway floor, surfing on socks all the way to the carpeted floor of the living room. Flicking on the television, a habit he hadn't broken or even become aware of, he entered the kitchen, turned on the kettle, and rummaged through the cupboards for his breakfast.

He fried two eggs and two rashes of bacon, layered them between two slices of toast, squirted on a dollop of ketchup and dug in, walking and eating on his way to the living room. When he finished eating, he boiled the kettle for the second time and made himself a cup of black coffee, which he sipped as he sat on the sofa. His almost euphoric state of mind had decreased within the hour and settled into a generic feeling of satisfaction. He was still watching television and enjoying his third cup of coffee when the door sounded.

He answered it with a smile. Orange sunlight glared at him when he opened the door. The air was light and cool, the temperature mild and moderate, but enough to warm his skin in direct sunlight.

"Hello, there." The man in front of him wore a suit and held a clipboard. When he tilted his head to look down at the papers attached to the wooden board, Lee noticed a large bald spot on his head. "Mr. Lee, is it?"

Lee's smile began to fade. Strangers who wore suits and called you *Mr.* tended to want to sell you something. "That's right," he said bleakly.

The man held out his hand. "James Holdsworth," he said with a grin.

Lee looked indifferently at the hand, his arms folded across his chest, before turning his attention back to the suited man's face. "What do you want?"

"Just a moment of your time," the man replied, unperturbed.

With his arms still folded across his chest in a defiant, defensive manner, Lee nodded and raised his eyebrows.

"May I ask how long you have lived in this area?"

"How do you know my name?" Joseph suddenly wondered.

"Well," the man said in a jolly manner. "You *are* registered to vote, your details were provided by—"

"Vote?" Lee spat out the word with disgust. He looked the man up and down to confirm his suspicions. "You're a fucking politician aren't you?"

The smile dimmed on the man's face. "I'm your local member of parliament," he confirmed.

"*My* local member of parliament?"

"For this district, yes," the politician tried to regain his composure, clawing it back with each spoken word.

"I've never seen you before."

He laughed subtly. "Well, I don't make a point of meeting everyone in the area," he said with a chuckle. "I do my best to help out every member of the community, of course, but—"

"Uh-huh," Lee interjected disinterestedly. "I'm pretty sure I've wrote to you before." He remembered. "I was being harassed by the police, my local community, and the press. I wrote to you to ask for help."

"Unfortunately politics is a very busy lifestyle. I'm here now, perhaps I can help," he said in a practiced tone.

"You want to help *now*?"

Holdsworth nodded.

"You didn't give a shit a year ago when the people of this town, *your people,* harassed the fuck out of me, but you want to help now?"

Holdsworth grinned and nodded.

Lee frowned, released a long sigh. "There's an election coming up, isn't there?"

"Well, actually, yes there is." He coughed, quickly changed his tone, and produced a leaflet. "I wonder if I could show you this. We have some big changes in mind for this town; we have many schemes in—"

"I'm not interested."

"Perhaps I can help you with your problem?" Holdsworth offered. "I do apologize if I never replied to a request of yours initially. May I ask what it concerns?"

"Why are you door-knocking anyway? Isn't that below you?"

"Of course not, I always like to engage with my public."

"Yet you only engage with them when you want to be re-elected."

"You have a cynical mind, I see." His tone was pleasant, hoping to restore some friendliness to the conversation.

"Cynical? No. Realistic. As far as I'm concerned, all you politicians are a bunch of lying, cheating, crooked wankers. You spout a ton of bullshit about lowering taxes and crime and fixing the healthcare system, but when you get in power, you do bugger all about anything. We don't live in a democracy any-more, we have the right to vote, fair enough, but what exactly is the point? It's always a vote between dickhead number one and dickhead number two. Which one are you?"

Holdsworth's face contorted into a mixture of confusion and regret. "I'm running on behalf of the Liberal Demo—"

"Ah," Lee interrupted, nodding. "A lib dem. That would make you dickhead number three. You see, you're just the same as dickheads one and two, you just share a few, ever-so slight differences of opinion. One likes fish and chips. Two tucks into some bangers and mash. You lot prefer salad. You all still eat out of the gutter."

"I'm not sure I understand."

"You're a bunch of useless, cheating, conniving—"

"Look, Mr. Lee, I didn't come here to be insulted—"

"Then you shouldn't have fucking come here, should you? I didn't ask you to. I hate you people. You make me sick."

Anger and frustration was building inside the MP but he did his best to push it aside. "Clearly you won't be voting," he said as calmly as he could.

"That depends."

"On?"

"The way I see it, all politicians are one of three things: liars, crooks, or pricks."

"I disagree."

"You would, but you have to be one, or all. I'll make you a deal, if you tell me which, I'll promise to vote for you."

The MP sighed and nodded to himself. "I really think I should be going now, Mr. Lee," he said in a defeated tone. "It was nice talking to you."

"A pleasure I'm sure."

James Holdsworth walked solemnly across the short driveway before disappearing around the corner, on his way to pester the neighbors.

A loud voice blasted across the silent street, immediately grabbing Lee's attention and making him jump: "Good morning!"

Riso Lechnen stood on his driveway with his hands on his hips. Lee acknowledged the Austrian with a welcoming wave and they both walked toward each other. They met at the end of Lee's driveway.

"Hey Riso," Lee grinned as he shook his neighbor's hand. "How's things?"

"Good, good," he boomed. His eyes traced the path that the MP had taken. "Who was that, what was he trying to sell you?"

"Bullshit," Lee answered.

"What?"

"He's a politician."

Riso nodded. "I'll ignore the door if it rings," he noted. "I came out to have a look at the damage." He gestured toward his garden. "It's going to take a lot of time and effort to sort all of that out. You haven't changed your mind since last night I hope?"

Lee glanced at both of the gardens; it would certainly be tedious work but he didn't have anything better to do. Part of him actually relished the idea. "Of course not, I'm ready whenever you are."

"Excellent! I need to make a quick trip into town, then I'll get the tools out of the garage and then we're set to go. Are you doing anything now?"

"No."

"Well, why don't you come over? Zala is in the house lying around. I'm sure she'll make you a cup of tea and I should be back in about ten minutes."

Lee looked behind him, the sound of the television echoed through the hallway and out onto the driveway. He had lost his state of euphoria, but perhaps Zala would help to restore it. "Sure," he agreed. "I'll just lock up and will be right over."

"I'll tell Zala you're coming, just walk right in."

12

The front door to the Lechnen house was ajar, the gap increasing and decreasing in the breeze. Lee popped his head inside and made his presence known with a welcoming shout.

No one answered.

He called again. "Zala, are you in here?" He walked straight into the house as he spoke, closing the door behind him and making his way into the kitchen. "Hello?"

"Hey!" She entered through the patio doors, a broad smile appeared on her face when she saw him. "I was just getting a deckchair ready outside, waiting for my day of relaxing." She planted a kiss on his cheek, a welcoming greeting he had become accustomed to over the last few days.

He grinned like a schoolboy when she kissed him and immediately turned his full attention to her. She wore baggy cotton pajama bottoms, blue and white stripes, and a pink tank top which clung tightly to her slender figure, exposing her voluptuous breasts and the tanned skin around her midriff.

"I may have to join you," he said as Zala glided across the kitchen floor, flicked on a kettle, and spun around, resting against the workbench. "Me and exercise don't go well together. Not without a struggle anyway. I'll probably be dead on my feet within minutes." He pulled out a stool from underneath the breakfast bar, spun it around, and sat down, facing Zala.

"You don't need to do much work." She had a twinkle in her eye. "Just make it look like you're doing something and Riso will end up doing all the work without realizing it." She chuckled. "When he's working and talking he loses track. That's how I got our last house redecorated. I just kept him talking, barely had to lift a finger."

"Thanks for the tip."

"What can I get you?" She stretched upward, standing on her toes. She removed two cups from the top shelf of a cupboard directly above the kettle.

Lee watched her back arch and her tank top lift, exposing more skin. "Tea," he said softly.

"Can I get you anything to eat?"

"No, I'm okay." He could feel the bacon and egg sandwich fighting digestion.

"Are you sure? I can make you a quick bacon sandwich if you want, maybe some toast?"

"I'm good, thanks."

Zala nodded and spun around again, enjoying the feeling of the wooden floor against her bare feet. Lee found himself quickly averting his lazy gaze. He had been staring lustfully and trance-like at her petite backside, his mind elsewhere.

He was relieved to see Zala's eyes on her hands and not on him. She handed him a cup of tea. "Two sugars, right?"

He took the steaming cup. He held it in both hands with his fingers wrapped around the white ceramic, soaking the heat into his palms. Zala paused near the counter and turned, an inquisitive look on her face. "Do you think I should change?" she wondered aloud, her eyes scanning her appearance.

Lee merely shrugged.

"I don't want all the neighbors to think I'm a slob, sunbathing in my pajamas." She clutched at the baggy thighs of her pajama bottoms.

"I didn't think you'd care. You don't strike me as the kind of person who pays attention to what others think."

Zala nodded, made a few humming and harring sounds, and then said, "I'm not, but from what you've told me, the people around here are quick to judge and love to gossip. One morning spent sunbathing in my pajamas could start a domino effect that ends with stories of the crazy Austrian woman who likes to dance naked around the garden."

Lee smiled as an image of a naked Zala merrily dancing around the garden popped into his head. "I think you're reading too much into it." He took a sip of his scalding hot tea and frowned at her above the rim of the steaming cup. "*Do* you dance naked around the garden?"

"*No,*" she said, stressing the word. "Not during the day anyway." She winked and Lee laughed. "I'll get changed if it rains," she concluded, resting back against the countertop. "The neighbors can gossip for the time being. Poor little suburban people. They work all day, come home, eat, sleep, and repeat. When the weekend comes around, the beers start to flow and the shit flies. Have you ever been to a neighborhood party?" she wondered.

Joseph shook his head and took another sip from the burning cup, which had reddened the palms of his hands.

"Our old neighborhood used to have them. Once a month, sometimes more. The snottiest, stuck-up neighbors would arrange and organize the barbecue and invite everyone in the street. There would be lots of food, much to drink, and lots to talk about. It was a communal thing."

"Sounds nice." He found the idea repulsive.

Zala shook her head. "It sounds great, but it wasn't. If you get together a group of strangers, all with differing ages, opinions, hobbies and cultures, people who only share geographical location, and you put all of these people in one place at one time, you know what they talk about?"

Lee searched his mind for a quick answer but one failed to materialize.

"They talk about the neighbors who didn't show," Zala confirmed. "Even if those same neighbors will be at the next barbecue or were at the last one. We still went to every party they had, though. I'd had enough after the first one but Riso couldn't turn down the free food and drink."

"So they never had the chance to talk about you?"

"They would have done it, individually. You don't need neighborhood parties to get neighborhood gossip."

"You seem to be quite the expert on these matters." Lee placed the burning cup down on the counter and rubbed his hands together, the heat from his palms brushed and tingled the skin on his arms.

"I find people fascinating." Her eyes wandered around the kitchen, searching for a clock. "Although some people I just find annoying." She made a mental note of the time from the digital display on the oven. "I was expecting to find neighbors and friends of both categories, in you I found the former, as for the rest of the neighborhood. . ." She allowed the sentence to trail off.

"They are—" Lee's words were cut short by the booming voice of Riso Lechnen.

"Hey!" the big man beamed as he strode through the house. "I hope you're ready to get dirty!" he declared, bounding through the house like Paul Bunyan.

13

The sun sat on a clear blue bed. Its ferocious rays stalked the world with an intense heat. With great exertion, Joseph Lee forced a heavy shovel into the muddy ground. The wooden handle scratched abrasively against his reddened hands, the metal head slicing easily into the dry gray mud. He applied as much leverage as his tired muscles would allow, opening the ground further.

With sweat beads forming on his forehead, dripping salty rivers down his face, he paused to catch his breath. He leaned on the handle for support, studying his surroundings. They had destroyed half of the garden. The top end had been turned into a mass of mud. All the grass, weeds, and dead flowers had been removed, along with the few levels of earth on which the deceased foliage sat.

After an hour of digging, both men noticed a flaw in their lethargic plans: they had no idea what they wanted the garden to look like. They didn't know the specifics of what they wanted to plant, where they wanted it and how much of it they wanted. Many mental pictures and blueprints had been created but nothing had been set in stone. They began without any direction and didn't want to continue that way and then discover that they had destroyed the garden beyond repair.

They came to a simple conclusion, requiring no immediate thought and allowing them to continue mindlessly: they would dig up the entire garden and deal with the re-turfing issues when they arose. They reasoned that as long as they didn't dig too deep and didn't damage the decking and paving slabs that adorned the head of the garden, they would be okay.

A few meters away from Joseph, Riso stood hunched over, his broad back—which looked like it would explode through his shirt and expose rippling green flesh—facing Lee. Riso's grunts and moans were constant as his tireless body worked without pause, his back muscles contracting and relaxing rhythmically.

Relaxing on the deck, her slender body reclined into a padded deckchair, her sunglasses and hair framing her face, rested the beguiling figure of Zala Lechnen. She had been there for the last hour and a half, putting her feet up as soon as the two men started digging. At her side, on a wooden table, was an ice-cold glass of lemonade. On the other side of the table, two slightly warmer pints of beer stood in wait for the busy workers who had been pausing to gulp down the liquid as often as they could.

Sitting up carefully, Zala took a small sip from her glass, her pursed lips kissing the cold rim. Her eyes met Lee's as she drank. She tilted her sunglasses and grinned teasingly at him. He was red raced, jelly legged, and breathless. And she knew it.

"Joseph!" she called. "Come over here." She pointed to an empty chair opposite her, waving him toward it. "Keep me company for a bit, would you? I want to ask you a few things and I'm sick of shouting."

Joseph immediately glanced at Riso, and the big Austrian, whose expression was completely unflustered, nodded. "Go keep her busy."

Relief swamped across Lee's face like a tsunami. He left the shovel in the ground and walked over the freshly dug earth, his weak legs trembling like petrified jelly. He crossed the decking and sat down, moaning in relief when his backside touched the stable seat.

Instantly a sensation of sedation swamped through his legs. He knew he wouldn't be getting back up again anytime soon.

He stretched and took some weight off his lower back, where a mild annoying twinge had developed over the last half hour. He also stretched out his legs and toes. The soles of his feet were bruised through repetitive digging; the action of pushing them down on the blade of the shovel was not only new to him, but it had quickly become painful. He dragged the chair near to the table where Zala sat, convincing his defiant legs that the small exertion would be worthwhile in the long run.

"You look tired," she noted from beneath her tinted glare.

"I am. It's been a long time since I've worked so much." He turned to look at Riso. The big man was still hard at work. "Riso hasn't even broken a sweat."

Zala said, "You should have said something. You've been struggling with that shovel for the last twenty minutes."

"I was struggling from the beginning." Lee laughed. "My feet were hurting after five minutes, and I wanted to quit after ten. I was hoping to continue until Riso started sweating, then I could have suggested that we take a break. He looks in high spirits. I didn't want to be the first to suggest giving up." He checked on Riso's progress as he spoke. The big man seemed to be enjoying his exertions.

"Even so, Riso would have just sat down for ten minutes, drank a pint or two, and then continued in even higher spirits," Zala said.

Lee nodded. "I was hoping to slip something into his drink."

"Like what?"

"Well, at first I was thinking Valium, maybe a sleeping tablet or two . . . " He turned to look at Riso when he spoke. "But he's a big man, and I'm not sure if he's drugable. How do you make a man that big go to sleep?"

"You have sex with him."

"With all due respect, I'd rather dig."

Zala laughed. Her exposed stomach rumbled gently from the vibration, and her breasts heaved with each respiratory exertion.

Joseph stared at her reclined, slender body. He found the urge hard to resist. She lay a mere meter away, her body stretched out, fully visible and framed by the sun. When he averted his eyes, he felt even more awkward, being resigned to absently stare at the patio door or the surface of the table. He couldn't see her eyes. They were shielded by the sunglasses. But as his eyes fell instinctively on her body again, he felt the need to justify his staring, adding dialogue to his wandering gaze. "You having a lazy day then?" His eyes were on her attire.

"Yep," she said happily. "Nowhere to go and nothing to do so there's not much point in dressing today. Not now anyway."

"Anything planned for later?" he wondered. He wasn't fishing for a date—far from it. He was tired and in pain, and a couple of painkillers and a long sleep was all he wanted.

"I might watch a film," Zala said unsurely. "I rented another one. I don't think Riso will watch it though. I was hoping he would tire himself out and have an early night so I could relax in front of the television with a glass of wine and control of the sofa." She lifted her glasses, tilted her head, and stared at her diligent husband. "But he never tires himself out. If you'd have drugged him, I wouldn't be in this mess."

"You think I should go back and help him?" He looked over his shoulder, watched Riso tear up another patch of grass, tossing the big slab of turf into a wheelie bin like it was a slice of toast. He didn't want to help and was pretty sure he was incapable of it, but empathy suggested he should at least try.

Zala shrugged, the soft skin around her neck creased and straightened, her breasts lolled to the side. Lee quickly decided that this was the best place for him.

"Maybe later," he reasoned.

—

Thirty minutes passed before Riso seemed to notice the idle worker. The ex-army man lifted his muddy face from a dust cloud of newly dug ground and stared at his tired neighbor.

"Have you had enough?" His voice boomed across the garden. He dropped his shovel and trotted over to the table. His chest rose and sank as he walked; his breathing was beginning to slip from its steady rhythm.

Lee nodded. His entire head had succumbed to sweat, heat, and fatigue. The front of his hair had formed a wet fringe and was sticking to his forehead, and the rest was beginning to mat. His forehead and cheeks, despite feeling like they were burning up, were clammy and cold to the touch. His legs gently pulsated and throbbed, and his back and feet had become numb and oblivious. He was relaxed, but he knew that the feeling would pass when he tried to work again. Or even stand. He'd needed to use the toilet for nearly twenty minutes but resisted the urge, preferring to stay seated.

"I'm completely shattered," Lee confirmed. The big man drained the beer in his glass and plonked it on the table.

"That's okay," Riso said, glaring down the garden through squinted eyes. "We've done most of the work. We can finish off another time."

Lee followed his line of sight. The garden had been completely demolished save a small strip of turf at the bottom, six feet long and spread across the entire width of the lawn. It would take them less than an hour to complete. What was once a mass of graying grass, blooming weeds, and dying flowers was now a field of mud, tumbled together with dead strands of greenery and numerous stones. It looked like a building site.

"Can I get you another beer?" Riso held up his glass and nodded toward the empty one in Lee's hand.

He smiled gratefully and passed the big man his glass. "Thanks."

Zala sat upright for the first time in over an hour, took off her sunglasses, and stared distastefully at the heavens. "Sun's gone," she declared, blaming the sky for letting it slip out of view. She set her sunglasses down and curled her legs underneath her.

Lee fidgeted uncomfortably in his chair, his full bladder making his tired movements even more awkward. Zala watched him squirm with a curious look on her face.

"Are you okay?" she wondered with an eyebrow raised.

"Just a bit sore," he said. He shifted again and then added: "And I need the toilet."

"Well, go."

"I can't be bothered to stand," he confessed, a statement his rebellious limbs backed-up.

"So you're going to just sit there and piss yourself?"

"If that's okay with you." He instinctively looked toward the house; in the kitchen Riso wandered around, snacking on a chocolate bar while retrieving two cold cans from the fridge.

"Do you want a bottle?" Zala wondered in jest.

Lee shook his head. "Just a sponge for afterwards."

"Go to the toilet, you lazy man."

Lee tried to stare her out before he eventually gave in. "Okay," he said, forcing his reluctant legs into action. "I'll give it a go." He stood slowly and made his way forward, dragging his legs as he walked.

"Are you drunk already?" Zala wondered, her eyes on Lee's intoxicated walk.

"I think my legs are; the rest of me hasn't caught up yet." He paused to stretch his awkward limbs, moaning with each elongation of his muscles, and then stumbled into the house.

He passed Riso in the kitchen—receiving a few smiles of sympathy for his pains—and made his way across the hallway and into the downstairs bathroom, a room barely big enough for a sink and a toilet. As he entered, he heard a mobile phone ring behind him. He drowned out the noise by shutting and locking the door.

After relieving himself and washing his hands, he unlocked the toilet door and stepped out. He had a problem trying to flush the toilet, the handle was completely unresponsive. He had given up after five attempts. As he walked back into the hallway, a direct line to the kitchen, he heard Zala and Riso speaking, their voices blasting through the kitchen and vibrating off the hollow walls in the hallway.

"How did he get your number?" he heard Zala say, her voice surprisingly harsh and toxic, hissed in a venomous whisper.

"I don't know." Lee recognized worry in Riso's voice for the first time.

"And he threatened you?"

"He tried to intimidate me, he seemed pretty urgent," Riso deliberated. "He said he would take legal action."

"Legal action?" Zala's reaction was one of surprise.

"He suggested a few other things, as well. Either way, he *knows*. We have to act quickly."

"It's too early." Zala snapped back, beginning in English and then breaking into her native tongue. Lee didn't catch any of it. They bounced more foreign words around. Lee slowed his footsteps. Their voices grew louder as he nudged closer to the kitchen.

"We'll be okay," Riso assured in English, his voice softer. "Just relax."

Lee's lazy leg strayed and his foot clipped the top of the skirting board. A scraping noise interrupted his eavesdropping. Thinking fast and not wanting to seem like he was listening in, he strode into the kitchen.

The Lechnens' stood next to each other. They had been embracing but broke away in Lee's presence. Shock came and went on Zala's face and, after exchanging a quick glance with Riso, she smiled at Lee. "I didn't hear you there," she said, her voice soft and calming again.

"The toilet wouldn't flush," Lee said, hooking a thumbing over his shoulder. "Is everything okay?" he wondered.

The couple looked at each other, many contemplations and conversations crossing between their glances before Zala spoke. "Just a few financial problems," she said with a protracted sigh. "It's a long story."

"Here you go, big man." Riso handed Lee his glass, filled to the brim with cold lager.

"Come on," Zala ushered. "Let's see if we can get drunk before the sun goes away completely."

"Sounds like a good plan," Lee agreed, following.

"One or two couldn't hurt, I guess," Riso uttered. He was still standing in the kitchen, watching the other two disappear outside.

"Huh?" Zala mumbled, turning to her husband.

"I have to go and meet Barry in a couple hours, and I don't want to be caught driving drunk," he explained to his wife before turning to Lee. "Sorry," he said sympathetically, holding his hands up in a submissive gesture. "I promised I'd go over to a friend's place tonight and help him out with a few things."

"That's okay," Lee said, watching a cloud of relief spread across Riso's rough features.

"We can get drunk and merry together another time, right?"

"Of course."

14

Joseph Lee watched the sun go down with Zala Lechnen sitting beside him. Together they watched the world turn from a dusty red to a murky gray before a blackness enveloped the skies. Riso had disappeared inside the house during the red dusk. While Lee and Zala contemplated the burning skies and the phrase *red sky at night sailors' delight, red sky in the morning sailors' warning* with their usual lighthearted humor, Riso was getting showered and ready.

Lee had noticed an odd change in Riso after the phone call. He seemed distant and preoccupied. He was still his ever-pleasant self, but for once Lee noticed a fault in that pleasantness. His niceties seemed fake and transparent, his kind words scripted, spoken by a man who knew what to say and how to behave but had more important things to worry about.

When Riso stepped into the garden, he was wearing a padded jacket and swinging a set of car keys around his forefinger and thumb. "Well, I must get going," he declared to the two night watchers.

Zala turned half-heartedly toward him. "I told you not to wear that," she studied his appearance with revulsion.

Riso looked down at his coat. "Why not? I only have two coats and this is the warmest." He continued to swing the car keys as he spoke.

"It's a padded jacket!"

"So?"

"You're already padded. You look like the Michelin Man."

Riso shrugged off the comment and turned his attention to Lee, who was staring at his attire with a smirk on his face. "I will probably see you sometime next week. I'll let you get some rest before we finish off the garden." His voice was warm, but his expression was distant.

"Okay." Lee was relieved that Riso hadn't asked to finish things the next day.

"Don't forget, we have your garden to do, as well," he reminded him, taking away most of Lee's relief. "Look after yourself." He winked at him, kissed his wife on the cheek, and then walked back through the house, waving at them with the back of his hand.

"What car does he drive?" Lee wondered as he waited for the sound of a car engine to spark into life. "Doesn't he drive the Merc?"

"No," Zala said, her voice was so gentle it almost disappeared in the wind. "We have a little Ford in the garage. It does most of the running around." She sighed pleasantly, a soft yawn escaping her lips.

Sitting up straight on the chair, she rested her arms and elbows on the table before laying her head on top of them. "I'm sorry he had to leave."

"That's okay. I'll have to go myself soon. I've never been so tired." He rubbed his hands as he spoke; the stinging in his extremities had disappeared. Flecks of hardened skin and small blisters were breaking through the red.

Zala smiled. "Do you want me to get you any painkillers? You're looking a bit stiff."

"No, thanks, I have some codeine in the house."

"How did you manage to get them?"

"I got a bunch a while ago for a dental problem . . . barely used them."

"What was wrong?" Zala wondered.

"I was in agony, that's about all I know," Lee confessed. "One tooth was driving me mad." He pushed his index finger into his mouth and pointed to a line of teeth at the back—a clear and evident gap exposed itself at the tip of his finger.

"Did they pull it out?" Zala asked, unable to hide a look of distaste.

"No. I did." He grinned sadistically, anticipating her reaction.

Zala cringed and quickly lifted her head. "You pulled it out *yourself?*"

Lee nodded. "It all happened during . . . " he paused, not sure how to phrase his words. "The awkward time." He settled upon. "I wasn't leaving the house much so I had no intention of going to the dentist. I wasn't really in touch with my doctor and didn't want to go through the hassle of getting another one so I ordered some painkillers online. I think I had about five orders, all for different opiate painkillers. I'm not up on the drugs culture, but I figured if I had five strong painkillers, one of them was bound to do the trick. As it turned out, four of the sites scammed me and I only ended up with one of the prescriptions."

"The Internet is a haven for con artists and scammers," Zala noted plainly.

"Yep. I think I had an inkling, but I was still suckered. Worth the risk anyway."

"That's a big risk though, isn't it? They could have taken your credit card and run, all for some painkillers?"

"They didn't have my credit card details. It was a third-party thing, online payment providing . . . services . . . " he said, stumbling. "Or whatever they call them."

Zala nodded in recognition. "So what happened, what did you do?" Her curiosity had taken hold.

"I took the codeine they sent me," Lee recalled. "Just one dose knocked back with a few glasses of whisky. Before long, I was as happy as Larry and high as a kite."

"I thought you could only be one or the other," Zala said wryly.

"I was every uplifting phrase in the book, and after I ripped my tooth out I was hopping mad and dancing on the ceiling before I was sleeping like a log."

Zala grinned. "How did you pull it out?"

"Pliers," Lee said abruptly, bringing a look of revulsion to Zala's face.

She made a noise of empathetic pain and disgust. "How did you manage? The back teeth go really deep, don't they? You can't just rip it out . . . can you? I mean they have huge roots, just as big as the teeth . . . don't they?" The questions were spat like gunfire.

"I found that out after I started." He cringed at the memory. "I was tugging at it for about ten minutes. I had to yank it back and forth to get leverage. I tried yanking it straight out but the pliers slipped. I lost control, they flew upward and I busted my nose on one of the handles. After a good amount of twisting and pulling, it popped out."

"Oh my god." Zala's face was a picture of horror.

"It cracked and chipped a lot on the way out," Lee continued, grinning at Zala's reaction and feeling a desire to disgust her further. "I was spitting blood and saliva and little bits of enamel. I used up a full bag of cotton buds getting rid of the blood. I was practically eating them toward the end."

Zala had her hand around her mouth as if she was feeling the same pain. "Did you pass out? Were you okay?"

"I was fine," Lee said pleasantly. "The painkillers and the alcohol took the pain away. I was a little put off by all the blood but other than that I was fine." He recalled something else and almost shuddered at the memory. "The morning after was a nightmare, though. I woke up on a blood-smeared pillow feeling like my mouth was on fire. I swallowed some codeine, waited for them to kick in, and then fell asleep again."

"Have you been to see a dentist since?" Zala wondered. The revulsion was fading but she still had a hand over her mouth, as if the problem was infectious and her hand was a barrier against the disease.

Lee merely shook his head.

"You're crazy."

Lee grinned. "So are you," he said with a wide smile that purposely exposed the toothless hole. "That's why we get along so well."

15

As darkness dripped its way across the sky, blacking out the afternoon, Joseph Lee and Zala Lechnen made their way inside. Both of them were tired, Lee's muscles ached, a sharp pain stabbed at his lower back, and an awkward twinge ran up his forearm whenever he moved it. Zala, who hadn't contributed to the backbreaking gardening, was softly sedated, her face peaceful, her eyes dreamy and distant.

They spoke for a while in the Lechnens' cozily decorated living room. Lee sat slouched on a leather recliner. Zala curled up on the sofa, her hands clasped together behind her head. She watched Lee through sleepy eyes, swapping conversation with him while a hushed television ran the evening news in the background.

After ten minutes of watching the peaceful Austrian, Lee said his good-byes and reluctantly climbed to his feet. When he closed the front door behind him and took his first few steps into the night, a relaxed sensation swarmed over him. His jellied legs felt almost euphoric against the soft breeze. His aching chest and tired lungs welcomed the wind.

His legs weren't entirely mobile and he realized that, to a spectator, he probably looked like he had soiled himself, but there was no one to spectate. As if to confirm his thoughts, he quickly glanced up and down the street, picking out the halos of light in and around the various streetlights and the beaming glows that radiated from active houses and whitened the street.

The expansive estate seemed empty and silent. Tall trees and shrubbery decorated the gardens. A few upstairs windows were visible, blue flashes from televisions flickered and buzzed. A soft red light wrapped warmly around curtains.

In the garden of Lee's next-door neighbor, a small blue orb beamed out a faint light from the center of a fountain, the light emphasized the swirling water as it cascaded over the lip of a stone edge and collected in a marble basin. The fountain and the water it spewed was the only visible thing in the garden. The small light failed to expose anything else.

A streetlight further down the road, a firefly in Lee's vision, flickered erratically like the glowing ember of a sucked cigarette before quickly brightening and then popping out.

Lee paused on the Lechnens' driveway, halting before crossing the empty street. A strange sensation of being watched crept over him, and he realized that the street wasn't as empty as he first thought. Out of the corner of his eye, he noticed a car—its color grayed by the night—parked ten meters away from his own driveway. The car was in a dark spot, between the halos of two streetlights, shrouded in a black sheet.

He squinted at the vehicle. Through the windshield, he saw the black-on-black of a silhouette. Unsure of its authenticity at first, his fears were confirmed when the figure twitched into movement.

His tired and sedated mind left his eyes to stare. Nothing moved fast enough in his brain to tell him otherwise or instruct him to a different action. The longer he stared the more movement he noticed and the better his eyes adjusted. Someone was definitely in the car. He wasn't sure if it was a man or woman, if they were young or old, but someone was there and they were staring right back at him. He shut his eyes and turned his head, snapping out of the trance. He rubbed his eyes with a brush of his thumb and forefinger, ignored the car, and crossed the street.

A suggestive niggle played around in his mind as he strode across the road, stepping in and out of the glowing orange circles. The street was empty and devoid of life, so who was the car waiting for?

As he stepped onto the path, walking parallel to the vehicle hidden in the darkness, a paranoia crept through him. The entire right side of his body tensed, as if expecting a sudden attack. Thoughts of being jumped from the side or being crept upon from behind forced him to quicken his steps. An irrational part of his brain declared that the more he worried about the situation, the more likely it was to happen. By the time he reached his front door, he was surprised not to have been jumped.

Before sticking the key in the lock, he turned back sharply, allowing the potentially stalking figure no time to hide, and quickly scanned his driveway. No one was there. No one was following him.

"Crazy paranoid fuck," he muttered under his breath as the irrational dispersed and the relief of reality came back to his racing blood and pounding heart.

He struggled with the front door, aiming the key with drunken arms and tired eyes. He opened the door, rushed across the threshold. Inside the house, his paranoia took no chances and he immediately slammed and locked the door.

Happy to have returned home, content with the end of a pleasant day, he dug out the bottle of codeine from a bedroom drawer, swallowed two of the tiny tablets, and then flopped on the couch with the television on. Within half an hour, his pain had faded to a mere background annoyance and a blanket of warmth had wrapped itself around his mind. He lay flat with his hands folded across his stomach.

A gentle pressure sat between his eyes and seemed to push at them from behind. He allowed the pressure to take control and soon felt like his eyes had grown warmer. The world they perceived also grew warmer. Everything he looked at was framed in a hazy glow of static.

His soothing blood pushed through every artery, warming every inch of skin and caressing every nerve while gently massaging his muscles. His head floated away, and his world made a momentary, pleasant slip between imagination and reality. A threatening thirst lingered at the back of his throat, a dire request for water, which he ignored with surprising ease. Soon all his spare thoughts—thirst, toilet, hunger—merged into one meaningless thought, which was ushered into a pleasant void. He remained there for an indeterminable time.

An incessant opiate itch swarmed over his body, a tingly and prickly all-over itch that wasn't welcome but wasn't entirely uncomfortable either. It felt like something very small was vibrating very fast all over his skin.

He ran his hands repeatedly over his face. It had been the only part of his body that hadn't itched but now that his hands brought attention to it, it itched. He rubbed away the tingly sensations and reveled in them, like someone waking up after a peaceful night's sleep would revel in the first stretch of the day. He scrambled to his feet and made his way to the toilet. The painkillers had taken away the urge to urinate, but underneath the barrier of opiates, he knew his bladder was in need of relief.

After relieving himself and staring mindlessly at his own reflection, he moved to his studio where the sensation of warmth increased, accentuated by the art on the walls and the beautiful star-filled night sky exposed through the wide windows.

As he looked out of the windows, he noticed there wasn't a single cloud in the sky, nothing to shade the stars and obscure them from view. A brighter flashing object then pulled his attention away from the heavens.

At first he noticed the light as it bounced against the glass, seemingly embedding itself in the window and looking like another star in the sky. It took Lee a few seconds to realize that the new star was actually a reflection. Following the source of the light, his heart skipped a beat when he traced it to a police car parked opposite his house.

The driver's side door had been left slightly ajar. A light was on inside the empty vehicle, spilling out into the road. The path of light traced along the driveway of the Lechnens' house. A policeman stood in the open doorway, his broad shoulders and bold uniform prominent in the glow. Walking closer to the window, brushing his sleeve across the glass to remove a smear of breath, Lee strained his eyes to see past the authority figure.

The police officer shuffled to the side and Lee's heart skipped again when he saw Zala Lechnen standing there, still dressed in her pajama bottoms and tank top. He watched her speak to the policeman for a few minutes. The policeman shifted from left to right, leaned back and forth, and adjusted his feet numerous times. Zala never moved. She was standing to the left of the door, gently leaning on the frame, her arms across her stomach as if she was trying to wrap herself up, sheltering from the night air that rushed through the open door.

The officer left and Zala closed the door. He trotted back to the car and clambered behind the steering wheel. He sat in the light of the car for a couple minutes, then he spoke into a radio or a phone, started the car and drove silently away.

Within seconds, the street was empty again. The stars had established their position as the main focal point out of Lee's high studio windows, but his intoxicated attention remained on the street. At first he looked for the car he had seen earlier. It had worried him, made him paranoid, but since entering his house and taking the narcotics, he had completely forgotten about it.

The car was nowhere to be seen.

Lee noticed that all the downstairs lights were on in the Lechnans' house. When he left the house, Zala was watching television with nothing but the light from the screen to accompany her. He could now see her silhouette pacing back and forward in front of the window, looking lost, troubled even.

Initially he feared for Zala—the police had just been to her house and now she was pacing up and down in front of the television with all the lights on—but his worries soon faded when the opiate sedation increased. Everything else vanished as he receded further into his own little world.

16

Joseph Lee dreamed of a big analog clock, framed with a circular border. The clock face was white, the hands that marked the time were scythes, vicious curled blades that shimmered. Standing at either side of the clock were two dark figures wearing black cloaks and expressionless faces. They held a scythe each, with the blade hanging over the clock and serving as the free-moving clock-hand. The second hand moved in a stuttered, random way, and each movement coincided with a strange knocking sound.

He woke up with that image still in his mind and the sounds still fresh in his ears.

His mouth was dry, furry almost. A nagging pain pricked the back of his head while a brick seemed to have lodged itself in the front.

He jumped when he heard the ominous knocking sound again. It took his brain a few seconds to realize that someone was at the front door.

It was after noon. He had been in his happy slumber for more than ten hours.

He exhaled slowly. He rubbed his eyes, stretched his drained muscles, and rose to his feet. The caller knocked five more times before he dragged himself out of the living room and answered.

He spoke with a cracked voice, "Hello." His eyes glanced over his own doorstep, his fuzzy vision finding it difficult to look into the glare of early afternoon.

"Joseph!" Zala's voice filled with relief, delight, and agitation. Lee forced his weary eyes upward and tried to focus them on the beautiful Austrian. "I wasn't so sure if you were in. I mean, I knocked and I knocked. I thought maybe you had gone to the shops but I knew you didn't drive and I didn't think you'd walk." She spoke quickly and without pause. "Something has happened. I need to speak to you, can I come in?"

Lee's eyes slowly regained focus. He noticed a bedraggled look of anxiety on his neighbor's face. The whites of her eyes were peppered with bloodspots and framed with a blackness that indicated she'd had very little sleep. Her hands were clasped in front of her. She rubbed them together anxiously, brushing sweat from one to the other.

"Sure," he said unsurely, stepping aside and tiredly motioning for her to enter.

She strode past without a second thought and stood behind him as he closed the door. She shuffled her feet as she stood, shifting her weight from one leg to the other and back again.

"Are you okay?" Lee closed the door and turned to face her.

"I . . . I . . . I," she stuttered helplessly, her eyes unable to focus on Lee's gaze. They moved all around his face, from his hair to his chin. He rubbed his eyes with the sleeve of his sweater before returning them to Zala. When he did, she was no longer looking at him and was staring at her own jerky feet.

"Come on." Lee reached out and took her by the arm, hoping to escort her into the living room and sit her down. As soon as his hand touched her elbow, she exploded, throwing herself at him, wrapping her arms tightly around him. She began to cry uncontrollably.

Lee wasn't a particularly comforting person. He liked to live his life away from people and their problems, but he reacted compassionately to Zala's tears. He wrapped his arms around her and pulled her slender body close, lowering his face within inches of the top of her head.

She shuddered as he held her, the tears pouring out of her eyes and onto his shirt. He wasn't sure what to say, what to do, or even what was wrong. His brain was still waiting for all cylinders to fire.

She seemed content enough to cry into his clothing and he was more than happy to hold onto her. He looked at the top of her hair, noted how unkempt it was. Normally it was gloriously wavy and glossy, but it looked bland and frayed. Her head bobbed as he stared, coming within touching distance of his nose. He instinctively sucked in a breath and noted a displeasing oddity. Her hair didn't smell bad and certainly wasn't pungent; it just didn't smell at all. He found himself sucking in deep lungfuls, trying to catch a hint of fragrance.

Eventually her sobs died down and she shook less in his arms. He released his grip on her slightly, ready for her to step back. But just as he did so another explosion of cries erupted from her. He pulled her closer. He let her cry, then pushed her away, holding her at arm's length. He stared into her sad eyes and she returned his gaze with a look of desperation.

"What is it?" he pleaded, feeling a deep sadness when he looked at her.

Her eyes crisscrossed again. They looked at Lee briefly before making a quick and hasty detour to the floor. She spoke in a soft, deep voice, filled with remorse. "It's Riso." These two words were broken by sobs. "He's dead."

———

"I was waiting for him last night." Zala sat beside Lee on the sofa. His arm was wrapped around her shoulder. "I waited and waited . . . " She leaned in closer, her head resting below his arm. "He never showed up. I tried phoning him but he didn't answer." Her violent sobbing faded, more from dehydration and tiredness than anything else. Lee didn't doubt that in half an hour or so the tears would flow again. But for now, only occasional sobs and a stuttering breathlessness broke her speech.

She produced a handkerchief from her pocket and held it close to her face, allowing the soft material to soak up her sniffles. "I fell asleep watching television. The door woke me a couple of hours later. It was the police." Her voice cracked as she spoke. "They told me Riso had been involved in an accident. They said he must have lost control. He drove off the road, into a tree." She paused, capturing soft sobs in the handkerchief. "He was doing seventy-five at the time. He died instantly."

Lee didn't know what to say. He scooped Zala into an embrace. Despite her strong appearance, her body seemed fragile and almost breakable in his grasp. He rested his chin on the top of her head. "I'm sorry," he muttered sincerely.

"I was up all night." Her words were muffled underneath Lee's clothes. "I don't know what to do."

Lee opened his mouth to speak but promptly shut it. He didn't know what to do either.

"I left the house through the night. I took the car out. I walked the streets . . . I just didn't want to be in that house. It was *our* house, it was *supposed* to be our house. Now it's just . . . "

"It's okay," Lee said.

"I keep running things over in my mind, what if he hadn't been drinking? He might still be alive. I know he didn't have much but they say even the smallest amount . . . " She pondered morbidly. "Maybe he was rushing back to see me, knowing I'd be worrying about him."

"It wasn't your fault," Lee assured. "Blaming yourself will only make things worse."

"There's no one else to blame."

Lee shrugged. She had a point. "Why don't I pour you a glass of wine? Help take your mind off this." He immediately regretted the offer. Somehow it didn't seem the right thing to say and he didn't think a depressant was the best thing to console a grieving widow.

Nevertheless, Zala nodded. "Okay," she agreed. "It is a little early but I suppose . . . " She finished with a round of breath-choking sobs.

Lee quickly shuffled into the kitchen, his mind in absolute chaos. He didn't like crying women and he certainly didn't know how to deal with them, but Zala had no one else to turn to. She only ever spoke to her husband and to Lee. Now she could only speak to Lee.

"Wine, wine, wine," he muttered under his breath as he hurried around the kitchen, Zala's sobs echoing through to him. He found a bottle of wine, red, dusty, old. He rummaged through one of the drawers, plucked out a corkscrew, and worked the twisted metal into the bottle.

He pushed the bottle between his legs, gripped the cork-screw handle, and pulled hard. He struggled, forcing his tired muscles to work, before it finally popped open. As the cork was wrenched out of the bottle, a small fountain of wine followed, inevitably spilling all over his crotch.

"Is everything okay?" Zala's broken voice called from the living room, failing to keep a constant tone and pitch.

"Just a little spill," Lee shouted back. "I'll be with you in a minute." He grabbed some kitchen paper and pressed it against his crotch. He retrieved two tall glasses, filled them with wine, and carried them into the living room.

When he entered Zala's line of sight, she turned to him and laughed. A subtle laugh at first, but enough to break through the tears. This transformed into a laugh of mild hysteria or maybe relief. Lee wasn't quite sure why she was laughing so he merely smiled back and continued to walk toward her.

He was meters away when he noticed that her gaze was on his crotch. She was still laughing when he handed her a glass of wine. When he went to sit, he realized why.

A big square patch of paper towel had stuck to the front of his jeans like tape. Further pieces of paper had flopped down, and one had tucked its way between his legs and up against his backside, the other flapped down his thighs. All the paper towels were soaked through. He looked like he was wearing a makeshift diaper and had soiled himself.

Noticing that the twinkle in her eyes had retuned, Lee decided to laugh too, staring at his own crotch and flicking the wet diaper with his fingertips. "My boxer shorts are in the wash," he said with a grin. "What do you think of men in nappies?" He posed for her.

Zala placed her glass on the floor to prevent it from spilling as her body shook with laughter.

Lee watched her with a smile. She laughed out of relief, relief that she had found someone to talk to and relief in the knowledge that he might help her. After a few more moments of parading his paper nappy up and down in front of the sofa, Lee sat next to her and put his arm around her slender shoulders. "You'll be okay," he said softly. "I'm here if you need anything."

She pulled away and looked deeply into his eyes. For a moment, Lee thought she was going to kiss him and, for reasons unbeknown to him, he felt anxious about it. But, then she didn't.

She spoke through fatigued vocal cords. "Thank you. You're a good man." Her eyes darted away from his face momentarily before fixing back. "There is one thing . . . " She said unsurely.

"What?" Lee was willing to do anything she asked.

"I don't want to go back to the house. Not now anyway . . ." she paused, her eyes dropped.

Realizing her mood was on its way back down, Lee quickly interjected, "You can stay here." She rediscovered her smile. "You can stay for as long as you want."

———

Lee made plenty of small talk, not just for her sake but for his own, too. He didn't want her to start crying, didn't want to see her upset. She was on her second glass of wine before the conversation reverted to her husband.

"I don't know what I'm going to do without him," she said solemnly.

"You're a strong woman." She seemed all cried out. "I'm sure you'll manage."

"He was so sweet. He looked after me. I have nothing now."

"You have your health." Lee cringed at his own words. He didn't know how to comfort people and hated it when he found himself reciting textbook sympathy, most of which he had pulled from movies.

"He looked after me. The house, the cars. He was my life."

"You can make your own life. You're a very intelligent woman."

She smiled timidly. "I'm not independent enough. I like to read, to study and to learn. I know enough to secure a well-paid job, but I don't think I could actually do it. I'm not the working type."

"I know what you mean."

Zala smiled at him. "I guess we are the same in that way."

Lee nodded. "When I lost Jennifer, I thought everything was over—she provided for me. She gave me a life that meant I didn't need to work. I was allowed to do what I wanted and accept everything as a personal achievement and not as a marker toward a greater goal—" he paused, his face twisted. "Does that make sense?"

"Not really," Zala said with a laugh, "but I understand what you're trying to say."

"You can cope. You're a stronger person than I am, and *I* managed to cope."

Zala frowned and looked at him questionably.

"Okay." Lee held up his hands. "*Eventually* I coped."

Zala's eyebrows were still raised.

"Okay, so I didn't cope. But you're stronger than me."

She laughed and looked away, a grave expression on her face. "Maybe you're right."

"I *am* right, I'm sure of it. If not, you can always live here with me," he said jokingly, a small part of him hoping she would agree.

"Thanks." She sat back, curled her legs underneath her, and leaned into Lee. "I don't know what I'd do without you."

17

Zala Lechnen fell asleep in Lee's arms. Curled up on the sofa with her hand still clutching a wine glass, her reddened eyes had closed and her mind floated into a dream world.

They had been watching television in silence. Lee was tired, and just as he was contemplating a strong cup of coffee or a couple of caffeine pills, he noticed a change in Zala's breathing. It was heavier, sedate. Her body had also fallen limp, practically fusing with his.

Maneuvering slowly so as not to wake her, he shifted and gently rested her down. He took the glass out of her hand and put it on the floor before grabbing a soft cushion, which he propped underneath her head. He stood back, looked down at her, and smiled. She stirred gently in her sleep, moaning softly. Knowing she would wake in a few hours, Lee made his way upstairs. The large house had one guest room. It hadn't been used in a year and had rarely been used before then. It was musty, cold, and stale. He would give Zala his own room and spend the night in there.

He stripped the sheets in his room and picked up a few unsightly objects—a stray sock, an old sweater that hung from the door, caffeine pills on the nightstand and codeine pills in the drawer. He also closed the curtains, opened a window, and switched on a bedside lamp.

He switched off the main light, checked and admired the ambiance, and then headed for the ensuite, which he quickly checked over. He removed a damp towel from a radiator that didn't seem to be working and repositioned the bath mat and the toiletries.

He popped his head into the guest room. The double bed in the center of the medium-sized room was covered with boxes and clothes. The window to the room was blocked with a black blind, drawn and shuttered, hiding the room from the outside world.

A slice of light had managed to find its way through the blind, cutting through a small tear in the material. The ray of sunshine was like a dagger of light through the dark room, coming from the top of the window and stabbing downward toward the door. A million specks of dust floated inside the beam, refusing to settle on any of the already dusty surfaces. Reaching underneath the blind—fearing that light may spontaneously combust the room if he peeled apart the oppressive shutters—he opened the window, allowing the room to breathe. He checked the floor, patted the bed down, and then left.

He spent the next few hours in the bright studio, his hand working frantically on a blank canvas, his mind a whirr of creative thought. The sounds from the outside world couldn't penetrate the double glazed windows, and he had left the studio door open so he would be able to hear any movement from downstairs. He was ready to greet and comfort Zala when she woke.

His mind was still tired. His eyes struggled to focus. He also had trouble keeping track of his thoughts, so he banished them completely, letting his subconscious paint the pictures while his conscious sat idle.

He thought about Zala and Riso but, as with the death of Jennifer, he preferred not to linger on those thoughts. He had liked Riso; he was a kind, gentle man with a big heart and a posture to match. He was the ultimate friendly giant. His death was untimely. Days earlier, Lee had found himself pondering about the early demise of the giant Austrian, but he had banked on a heart attack being the culprit.

A battle had raged in his fatigued mind when Zala spilled her sorrows. His lust had fought his morals. Riso's demise would bring him closer to Zala and would give him the chance he needed to be with her, but the part of him that bonded with Riso, forming a happy friendship, countered the morbid, merciless lust.

The light in the studio grew dimmer and dimmer as his objectless painting progressed. The outside world turned an eerie gray and the light of the fading sun struggled to break through the tall windows. Lee snapped out of his sedated trance, stopped his painting, and stared out of the windows. The house next to the Lechnens' was bright and welcoming. Lights of orange, yellow, blue, and red flickered or remained constant out of four upstairs windows. The house was active, vibrant, alive, and against the disappearing sunlight, it looked like a pleasant safe-haven. Warming to the heart.

The Lechnens' house was a different scene altogether. It had a colder, less approachable look. It looked out of place. None of the lights were on and all the curtains had been left open. This, coupled with the tragedy that had befallen the homeowner, turned the building, and all mental images that accompanied it, into a wintry nightmare.

Staring at the bleak house, Lee could feel the imagery suck the happiness out of him, replacing it with a somber sense of tragedy. He wondered if that was how the neighbors saw his house, and how they had seen it since Jennifer's death. Because even though it wasn't empty, it was just as bleak, cold and lifeless. Gradually, all the streetlights flickered on, but the fluorescent glow did little to aid the sorrowful image and Lee dragged his attention away.

He looked at the mess he had created on the canvas and frowned, tilting his head this way and that, trying to decipher its chaotic code.

"What is it?"

The voice startled him. He quickly turned on his chair. Zala stood in the doorway, her arms folded across her chest, her shoulder leaning against the wooden door frame. Her eyes stared past Lee's shoulder at the fresh painting.

"I'm not entirely sure," he admitted. "I didn't hear you . . . "

"I have quiet feet," she said softly, her voice tired. "And you were too busy looking out the window."

Lee nodded. He couldn't see Zala's features from the front, but the glow from a hallway light framed her in an angelic silhouette. "I wasn't really painting anything," he explained. "My mind is a blank. I was just . . . " He turned toward the painting and stared at it momentarily before turning back. "Doodling, I suppose."

"Are all of your paintings like this?"

"No, this is just a one-off."

"Good because it's . . . " She checked Lee's expression before settling on a word she deemed inoffensive. "*Strange.*"

"It's horrible, you mean."

"I never said that."

"I know, but it is. I wasn't concentrating. I was waiting for you to wake up. I didn't want to watch television or anything in case I disturbed you, so I came in here." He motioned toward the painting. "This was painted to pass time."

Zala stepped forward, out of the framing light. She studied the walls next to the door and slapped a hand against them. "It's dark in here." She found the light switch and snapped it on. The light from the small bulb bounced off the white walls and exposed every niche of the open and expansive studio.

Instantly her eyes were drawn to the walls, a contorted look of awe, wonder, and amazement spread across her face as she admired the newly hung artwork covering the walls like wallpaper.

Lee followed her open-mouth gaze as she strolled around the room, keeping a steady distance from the paintings and side-stepping along, appreciating each one in turn. "I never did show you my work, did I?" he muttered.

Zala merely shook her head. She seemed lost in a trance, still admiring the wall of the studio where morbid canvases of painted dreams and delusions hung. "They're amazing," she said after a short awe-struck silence.

"You sound surprised."

"What's this one?" She stopped in front of a small canvas, painted with many shades of red, orange, and black. It was a slurry of gothic morbidity, a vibrant canvas that immediately captured the eye and the imagination.

"A sunset," Lee said placidly. "A *dying* sunset," he clarified.

Zala walked closer to the painting and lifted her hand to within inches of it, tracing a shape with her finger. "It's amazing."

"Thanks." Lee was starting to blush. Showing off his art made him unreasonably uncomfortable. "I painted it a few days ago." He watched Zala move her face closer. "I watched a program about the death of the sun and well . . . I took it literally." He let his self-conscious gaze fall upon the vibrant painting. It depicted a surreal sunset with the dying sun fading in the heavens, bleeding out its life across a dead landscape.

Zala moved on. "Do you give them names?" she wondered.

"There's not much point, I'm the only one who sees them."

Zala finished with the left wall. She crossed the room to study the many paintings that Lee had thought of as pointless. They depicted random and dull things: views, landscapes, magazine covers. Zala stared at them with the same amount of approval.

"You have an amazing ability," she noted.

"Thanks," said the blushing artist.

"They're so alive and exciting." She found a painting of the view from the studio windows, which depicted the Lechnens' house in the forefront. She walked closer to clarify her point. "Some are a little shabby, I'll be honest," she said as she quickly skipped past a bland landscape with a fiery sky. "You must paint quickly. How long did it take you to paint each of these, on average?"

"A few hours," he said with a shrug, delighted that Zala, like Jennifer before her, was impressed by his work.

She finished studying the second row and turned her attention toward Lee. She opened her mouth to speak but paused, her eyes on the wall behind him.

Lee was confused at first but he soon realized what had drawn her attention. His heart sank. He had devoted the wall behind him to his pictures of Zala. A wall of devotion that he'd completely forgotten about in his fatigued state.

Zala, her mouth still slightly open and her attention fixed, walked past him, closed the door to expose the wall fully, and then stood back to admire. Lee didn't dare turn around. He was mentally cursing himself and wondering which excuse, if any, he could use. In seconds, her view of him could transform from talented painter to twisted stalker.

For interminable moments, the room was silent. Lee slowly spun around on his chair and broke the silence. "Jennifer," he muttered in a soft tone. Zala was studying a group of pictures to the left of the door. "They're all pictures of her," he lied.

"You were right, she does look like me." Zala sidestepped across the rows of portraits. "You loved her a lot. It shows."

Lee nodded, feeling relieved. His eyes drifted along the rows of pictures to the end one, the biggest one. It was the one he had painted of Zala while she was sunbathing. The Lechnens' house was in the painting, standing tall behind the sunbathing goddess. He wouldn't be able to explain his way out of that one.

Before he could think of an excuse or a reason to pull Zala out of the room, her wandering eyes fell upon the painting and her legs followed. She stood directly in front of it, stared for what felt like hours. She spent more time looking at that one piece than she had all the other paintings in the room. Lee watched wearily, staring at the back of her head and hoping she wouldn't think him perverse.

"Amazing," she concluded, pulling away from the wall of paintings and standing alongside him. "You have a gift."

Lee waited for a *but*. He waited for the questions and comments, but when none came, he simply said: "Thanks."

"I don't know why you didn't show me earlier. If I could paint this well, I'd want to show it off to everyone I met." Her eyes spun around the room again.

Lee was lost for words. He wondered what she thought of the sunbathing girl, whether she realized it was her or not and, if she had, why she hadn't said anything. She bent down and planted a soft kiss on his forehead before raising her head and lowering her eyes to meet his. A sadness lingered there, a look of pity almost.

"Are you hungry?" she wondered.

"A bit."

"What do you want to eat? I'll cook us both something."

"I'm not . . . " He trailed off uncertainly. "Whatever you want," he said, noticing a twinge of happiness on her face. She was still sad, but she was all cried out.

"You do have food in the cupboards, don't you?" she asked.

"Yes."

"Okay, I'll go and see what I can do." She turned to leave, stopping in the doorway. "If I were you, I'd scrap that." She gestured toward the messy canvas. "Clearly you can do better."

"Will do."

He watched her leave. Her trousers hung loosely off her waist and flared out around her socks. She trod on them with every step as she walked across the carpeted landing. He listened to her soft footfalls on the stairs and waited for her to fully descend before he sighed to himself in relief.

He looked at the sunbathing painting. There wasn't much detail in her face. Lee hadn't really seen much of her face that day—the top half had been covered with hair and large-rimmed sunglasses, the bottom half had met with the glare of the sun—so most of the detail had gone into her sun beaten body. She may have not recognized herself as the centerpiece of the painting, but she surely would have recognized the house and the garden. The left side of the picture even showed the driveway and a partial slice of the silver Mercedes.

He shrugged the thoughts away, stood, and walked over to the large windows. He clasped his hands, raised them above his head and stretched, yawning deeply.

A black car, visible thanks to the moonlight and the radiance from nearby street lights, grabbed his attention. It was parked to the left of his driveway, opposite the Lechnens' house. He immediately tried to focus his eyes on the person sitting in the driver's seat.

He wasn't sure if the car was the same one he had seen the night before. He hadn't seen much, after all. But it was parked in the same spot and its grayed-out shape and dark contours matched the vehicle from the previous night.

As he strained to catch a glimpse of the man behind the steering wheel, a light suddenly burst on inside the car. Joseph jumped. The driver of the vehicle, wearing a full suit of black, including a black baseball cap and sunglasses, was staring right at him. He was looking up, his pale white skin ominous against the gray light.

A storm of fear and worry built up inside Lee. They continued to stare at each other. None of them moved. Lee didn't even dare twitch.

The man in the car slowly raised a gloved hand and pointed it at Lee, his finger aimed at him like an accusatory gun. He continued to watch as the hand moved to the man's neck. Holding there like a knife, the man made a swiping motion across his pale skin before he pointed back at Lee.

An incoherent, horrified mumble escaped Lee's lips. Anger and fear welled up inside of him. The urge to turn was more prominent than ever. But, before he could avert his eyes, the light inside the car flicked off, the driver's image now a block of pixelated blackness.

Lee took a step away from the window. His heart pounded inside his chest, his hands sweaty, his whole body agitated. He continued to stare out of the window, hoping to catch sight of the man again and maybe offer a few hand signals of his own, but the car quickly pulled away, disappearing down the street.

"Fucking weirdo," he spat, still standing at the window. "What the fuck was his problem?" he muttered to himself as his heart continued to race and his mind struggled to grasp an explanation.

He walked back to the easel, stared at the messy painting, shaking his head in distaste. Taking the sheet of canvas, he ripped it up into eight separate bits and dropped them into a waste paper bin. He then cleaned the palette of paint and washed the brushes thoroughly before heading out of the room, by which time the memory of the man in the car was just an annoying niggle stabbing suggestively at the back of his mind.

18

Lee decided to shower and change before heading down-stairs. The jets of hot water massaged his tired muscles and helped ease his fatigued mind. He thought briefly about the man in the car while standing underneath the hot streams.

Joseph could think of a number of reasons explaining his presence, but only one reason why he stared at him and tried to intimidate him: he was an asshole. From this, Lee deduced he was probably a local. Not many people in the neighborhood liked him, and each one of them would enjoy telling stories to their friends of how they threatened or intimidated Joseph Lee. It was a game to them. People had short memories and fickle minds, but after his encounter at the café, Lee realized that they still remembered, they still hated, and they would still make their dislike known.

As the hot water splashed over his face and began to wake him up, Lee also thought more about his current dilemma. Riso's death was sudden and would eat at Zala for years to come. His job was to help her get through it or to at least make it easier for her. He almost laughed when he came to that con-clusion. He had gone to pieces when he lost his wife. He hadn't left the house, lost all sense of personal hygiene, and generally went into self-destruct mode. He wasn't the best role model for coping with loss.

He did have strong feelings for Zala. She had helped him get his life back on track and he would make sure he returned the favor. Every time he thought about her and her current dilemma, he found his mind drifting away to a lustful, less sympathetic place. After all, she was the woman of his dreams. After Jennifer, he had resigned himself to thinking that he would never find anyone as amazing or as beautiful again, but Zala had all that Jennifer had and more.

After showering and changing, he made his way downstairs. His senses were struck by a beautiful aroma wafting from the kitchen and spread pleasantly through the house. Instantly his taste buds tingled, and he almost ran down the stairs, eager to see what Zala had cooked. She was in the kitchen, underneath a veil of steam and smoke.

"What are you cooking?" he wondered as he strode through the wall of steam.

Several pans were simmering away; vegetables, whole and chopped, waited inside a glass bowl on the counter where Zala stood. In front of her were several rashes of bacon, which she was cutting with a pair of scissors.

"Pasta," she said without turning around, her hands working the scissors with great speed.

"It smells good." He hovered over the pans to try to catch a glimpse of the culinary delights.

"It's one of my specialties. I used to cook it all the time for . . . " she trailed off and held her head low, taking a few seconds to breathe before she continued slicing the meat.

"I didn't know I had so much food."

"You don't anymore." Zala scooped up a mass of raw bacon bits and dropped them into an empty bowl next to the vegetables before washing her hands. "Tell me before you go shopping." She turned to look at him. "I'll help you out. You need a woman's touch, you have far too many ready-meals and cans. I mean, what is this?" She opened a cupboard above her head and removed a tin. "'*Full English Breakfast* in a can,'" she read the label before showing it to Lee, a look of disgust on her face.

"It's convenience food."

"It's dog food."

"It's quick and edible, that's what matters."

Zala shook her head and pushed the can back into the cupboard. "You need healthy, hearty, home-cooked food."

"I can't really cook."

"Learn, read some books, search the web, I'll even teach you. Just stop eating that crap," she hooked her thumb over her shoulder to the cupboard of convenience.

"Fair enough," Lee agreed happily. "So, when is it ready?" he licked his lips.

"Twenty minutes. Go sit down. I'll shout."

The dining room was on the other side of the house. It hadn't been used in a long time but had been cleaned during one of Lee's many frenzies. Unbeknownst to him, Zala had set the table, laying out a tablecloth, cutlery, and plates. She carried all the food to the table before calling for Lee to sit down.

"This looks amazing," he said in open-mouthed delight as his eyes pored over the food. The plate in front of him was piled high with pasta with a big dollop of sauce in the center. There was also a small basket of bread and a bowl of salad. "You didn't have to go to all this trouble."

Zala smiled and sat down opposite. "Do you want some wine?" She tilted the neck of a bottle of white wine toward him. When he nodded, she filled up an empty glass next to his plate before filling up a glass of her own.

They ate in silence, exchanging brief glances and smiles. Lee looked up at her after a while. "How are you?" he wondered.

She shrugged softly, her eyes on her plate.

"You can stay here as long as you want," he reminded her, tucking into his pasta.

"Thanks," Zala said. She stabbed her fork into a mountain of spaghetti and twirled it around several times before rejecting the crimson stained strands and opting for a tiny zucchini instead. She chewed the minuscule piece of vegetable as if it was made of rubber.

Lee noted her lack of appetite and frowned. "Do you have everything you need from the house for tonight?" he wondered.

"Hmm?" Zala looked at him as if she had just broken a trance.

"A nightdress, pajamas . . . do you need anything from your house for tonight?"

Zala shook her head. "I don't have anything with me, but it doesn't matter."

"Do you want me to pop over and get you something?"

Zala's features seemed to suddenly awaken. "No," she said hastily, anxiously, her features in a moment of disarray. "That's okay." She quickly calmed down and returned her bland stare to her plate. "I'll get what I need tomorrow. I have it all ready anyway. I laid out all of my belongings and packed my essentials into a suitcase before I came over."

"Why?" Lee asked, speaking with his mouth full and shooting breadcrumbs across the table. Zala didn't notice.

"To give me something to do, I guess," she replied distantly. "After I heard about Riso, I didn't know what to do but I knew I had to get out of that house. I guessed I would probably go to a hotel, just for a few nights." Her features changed again, sinking in on themselves. She dropped the fork she'd been idly twiddling and covered her face with her hands. She sobbed as she spoke. "I don't know what I'm going to do."

Lee instantly jumped to his feet, dropping a forkful of messy spaghetti. He rounded the table to comfort her. He wrapped his arm around her and squatted down to her eye level. "It's okay, you don't need to do anything."

"I have his funeral to arrange!" she spat through the cushion of her hands.

"There's no rush, you can go at your own pace. Wait a week or two."

"There's also the house," she continued, ignorant of Lee's reassurances as all her worries hit her at once. "It's in his name . . . they'll take it away from me."

"They can't do that."

"He has a mortgage, *had* . . . there are bills to pay. I don't have any money." She sobbed deeply, sucking in deep and quick breaths and trembling in his grasp. "I can't survive without him, he provided me with everything."

"It will all work out. I'll make sure of that."

She hugged him tightly, her arms wrapped around him like a belt. "Thank you so much," she cried into his shoulder. "I really don't know what I'd do without you, I know I keep saying it but . . . " she finished with a round of sobs.

He found himself worrying about the same things. Zala had helped him turn his life around; he had moved from a self-destructive hermit to a man who actually cared whether he lived or died, and all because he wanted to impress and please her, because he longed to be with her. Now he needed to use that new found confidence to help the woman who had given it to him.

He sunk into her and rested his head on her shoulders. He had impressed her and comforted her and he knew that, one day, after all the misery and memories faded, she would be his.

19

———

They said good night to each other just before midnight. They had sat down to watch a few films while the food settled, chatting all the way through. Zala recounted great times she had shared with Riso, all the good times and none of the bad. Lee had been by her side all the while, reassuring her when needed, but essentially just letting her talk. She had a lot of emotions to express and a lot of memories that were dragging her down; reciting them to another human being seemed to ease a great burden.

She had wanted a nightdress and asked Lee if she could borrow one of Jennifer's, correctly guessing that he had kept all of her belongings. Lee had packed them all into a box and stuffed them into the attic. He offered to lend her one of his own shirts—oversized, baggy, and stretched—which she graciously accepted.

He had a brief moment to admire her in the shirt, with her slender legs exposed, as she kissed him goodnight before retiring to the master bedroom with a glass of water. Lee was also tired. It had been a long day, one which began with a sedate hangover and ended with a new roommate and a dead friend.

He made his way into the guest bedroom and the guest bed. Lying on his back, he stared at the blackened ceiling and contemplated his current situation. The more he thought the more awake he felt, the more awake he felt the less he tried to think. He struggled to relax, his mind racing behind closed eyelids. He tried deep and steady breathing, he tried counting sheep. Nothing worked.

He decided against sleeping. His overactive mind made the decision for him. He climbed out of bed, slid his bare feet into a pair of slippers, threw on his T-shirt, and left the room. If he had trouble sleeping and shutting down an overactive mind, he reasoned that Zala would as well. She had more to contemplate and had napped during the day. He stopped in front of the master bedroom and pushed an ear to the door, hoping to pick up a sound.

He heard the soft patter of gentle, rhythmic breathing; interrupted by the cloudy thud of the thick bedroom curtain swaying in the breeze of an open window. He reached out his hand and gently laid it upon the door handle, cringing as he did so. He pushed down on the handle, cursing under his breath when the lock scraped against the wood and a soft creaking sound entered the hallway.

He waited for several seconds before he continued. He shoved the door handle all the way down, gently pushed the door open. Moonlight streamed in through an open window and spilled over the top of the bed. A crumpled heap, framed in the silvery glow, lay in the center. She was facing away from the door. Not wanting to enter the room, he merely stood where he was, watching. She was breathing softly but her breaths seemed to catch in her throat and croak on the way out. A day's worth of crying had torn her throat apart.

She was asleep, a day which had frustrated Joseph's mind and kept him awake had the opposite effect on Zala. Smiling at the sleeping heap, Lee retreated and gently closed the door behind him.

He stood on the landing momentarily, contemplating what to do. He thought about going back to bed and trying to sleep but doubted his brain was ready to shut off. He thought about watching television but it was past midnight and he doubted that shopping channels or soft porn would help him sleep. He also contemplated painting or writing in his studio but quickly remembered how he had fared earlier in the day—his mind felt even less creative now.

Walking back into the guest bedroom, he quickly climbed into a pair of jeans and threw a sweatshirt over the T-shirt. He then crossed the landing and headed downstairs, treading lightly. He began to aimlessly walk around the house, his hands stuffed in his pocket, his feet pointlessly pacing as he studied everything with the hope he would find something to do.

In the kitchen, he noticed a set of keys resting on the countertop. Three keys hung from a cute teddy bear keyring. He picked up the set of keys, tossed them from hand to hand. He remembered what Zala had said, that she had packed all of her belongings into a suitcase and left it at her house. She didn't want to go back; she found it cold, empty, and filled with memories. But she would need that suitcase.

Thinking the fresh air would do him some good, Joseph dropped the keys into his pocket and left the house. After he gently pushed the front door closed behind him, moving it inch by inch until it smoothly clicked into its frame, he turned to face the night. The cold air slapped his dry skin like a moist towel. His warm, tired body froze, and his breath turned to vapor.

He stood in the breeze, his eyes closed, enjoying and becoming accustomed to the rushes of cold air. Leaving the door unlocked—it would take a brave burglar with impeccable timing to rob him—he strode down the driveway. He felt his senses liven up, the dull ache that had stuck at the back of his eyes all day began to fade into a mere nuisance as his eyes adjusted to the blackness.

The neighborhood was silent. All the neighbors had gone to bed awaiting early mornings at work. The Lechnen house was also silent, although this came as little surprise to Joseph Lee. When he walked across the Lechnens' property line, skipping over the lawn Riso had had high hopes for but would now be left untouched, he noticed the Mercedes was missing from the driveway. The thought hit him as odd but he pushed it to the back of his mind and made a note to question Zala about it later.

He unlocked the door, shut it softly behind him, before dropping the keys in his pocket and making his way through the house. A little voice inside him told him not to turn on the lights. He wasn't sure why; there was probably only one person who would know whether he was a burglar or not and she was asleep in his house, but he listened to it nevertheless. His eyes had adjusted enough to the darkness for him to make it through the house with relative comfort.

He worked his way to the stairs and began to climb. On the third step, he missed his footing and clattered against the banister, just managing to stay on his feet. He gripped the banister hard as he made his way up the remaining stairs, nearly missing the final step before trying to climb an imaginary one.

Feeling his way around the landing, his back to the wall, he discovered that all the doors to the house were wide open, leaving too many opportunities to fall backward. At the end of the hallway, he found the master bedroom. He walked straight into the room and straight into the corner of a cupboard door, which swung from a hatch at head height.

He recoiled instantly, screeching in agony as the corner struck him in the center of his forehead. Tiny stars flashed through the darkness. He held his hands to his head, scuttled steadily to the bed—using his knees as a guide—and flopped down.

"Fuck!" His voice sounded like a foghorn in the darkness. "Fuck, fuck, fuck," he repeated angrily as a stabbing pain bolted through his skull.

He rubbed his eyes until the stars began to disappear, but he stopped abruptly when he saw a flash of yellow light quickly enter and exit his vision. It had shone through the bedroom window, lighting up the room before disappearing again.

The gentle roar of an engine sounded through the double-glazed windows. Lee rose to his feet to investigate. A large white van had pulled to a stop outside the Lechnens' house, its beaming headlights focused down the street. Lee watched curiously as the engine was flicked off and the lights faded. Blinking away the ferocious and sudden light, he continued to glare at the vehicle, parked horizontally in front of the driveway. Through the faint silvery glow of moonlight, he watched two men clamber out.

The one closest to the house, the driver, stopped to pull up his pants and admire the empty house. The second man slowly made his way around the van to join his friend. Lee's heart nearly jumped out of his mouth when he recognized the passenger. He had a huge build, tall and muscular with a shaven head and neatly fitting clothes.

His horrified eyes strained to focus on the passenger's face. "Riso?"

20

The driver disappeared around the back of the van, leaving the tall figure standing solitary. Lee knew that posture, he knew that pose. His curious eyes glanced at the driver. The smaller man had retrieved four big duffel bags from the back of the van. He handed two to his friend and kept two for himself.

Lee could only watch in bemusement and awe. He wanted to run but he had nowhere to run to; he wanted to hide but his muscles had seized from shock. He quickly glanced around the room. A line of built-in wardrobes covered the back wall, a small ensuite was a few strides away, and there was space to hide underneath the bed. Before he could attempt to drag his body into a hiding place the two men moved.

The big man moved first, quickly followed by the driver. Just as Lee managed to move his limbs, he heard the distinct sound of a key in a lock—the metallic sound reverberated through the empty house.

He stepped next to the bed but stopped before sliding underneath—curiosity got the better of him. He turned his ear toward the doorway and listened to the noises coming from downstairs where the two men conversed quietly, their whispers clear in the deathly silence.

"We need to make this quick and quiet," a heavy voice instructed.

"Quick yes, quiet no." The reply was spoken in a lighter tone, an English accent. "How are we supposed to be quiet exactly?"

"Just . . . just make sure you don't make too much noise, okay?" the heavier voice whispered, his words less fluent and more practiced, layered with a touch of anxiety.

"Fair enough, is this a nosy neighborhood?"

"No, but we can't be too careful. We can't have anyone see us. Come on, let's start upstairs."

Lee moved so fast that he didn't move at all, his body merely shuddered. He left his feet behind. Dropping to his knees, he grasped at the carpet and pulled himself underneath the bed, grateful nothing obstructed his path.

The footfalls of the two thieves seemed to vibrate through to him as they climbed the stairs, when in fact he was simply reacting in fear to every soft thud, his heart jumping erratically.

"You go clean out the office, I'll get the guest room," the man with the heavy tone instructed. "Make sure you get *everything.*"

The two men went their separate ways. Lee practically kissed the floor, staying as low as he could. He knew he had to get out of the house; if he could escape he could run across the road and phone the police. He cringed at the thought—he hated the police. They had made his life a living hell. A big part of him wanted to stay and find out if his assumptions were correct. He was sure the heavier man was Riso. He certainly looked like him and one of the whispering voices sounded like it was spoken with a foreign tongue.

Duffel bags ruffled as items were stuffed inside, some clinking and clattering on their way in. Each noise seemed to speed up Joseph's heartbeat and add another bead of sweat to his palms and forehead. He considered getting out from underneath the bed and running. Even in the dark, he fancied his chances of finding the staircase and making his way down safely, his night-vision had adjusted to that degree. He could be halfway across the road before either man had even realized something was wrong.

But both of the men were in rooms next to the staircase, and the master bedroom was right at the end of the hallway. They would hear him running and would probably step out of the rooms they were robbing and obstruct him, beating him to a bloody pulp. There was also a strong possibility that they would simply turn on the lights as soon as they heard a noise. They could grab him and pin him to the floor in a matter of seconds, simply turning the lights back off before finishing him off.

Numerous escape plans raced through Lee's head but they all ended the same and none of them were pretty. Regardless, he realized his body was moving, pushing itself out from underneath the bed of its own accord. He felt like he had drifted out of his body, and his rational mind stood over it, screaming obscenities at it, begging it to retreat, but the part of him that controlled his movements remained stubborn.

"Done!" one of the men shouted. The noise startled Lee's instinct and sent it crawling back under the bed.

Angry footfalls crossed the landing to meet with softer ones.

"I said be *fucking quiet!*" the heavy, foreign voice said in a venomous whisper.

"Sorry. I'm done; everything's in here." The cling and clatter of cluttered objects sounded as the man gestured toward his bag.

"Good, I'm just finishing up. Go make a start on the bedroom."

Lee's head dropped further to the ground, inaudible vulgarities screamed through his breath. He saw the shape of shins and feet as one of the men clambered into the master bedroom.

He wore heavy boots with thick heels that clunked against the floor as he walked, imprinting his boots into the soft carpet.

He opened up the built-in cupboards and began stripping the clothes out and stuffing them into a duffel bag on the floor. The thief whistled while he worked, breaking into the theme from *The Great Escape* as he plucked clothes from the wardrobes.

The second man stormed in seconds later, his heavy boots thudding against Lee's heart.

"Shut up!" he ordered instantly.

"I'm just whistling."

"I told you to be quiet!" Lee strained to hear the voice and decipher its identity.

"Will you relax, no one can hear us. Every fucker on this street is asleep."

"Just in case."

The whispers gradually faded. Lifting his face from the floor, Lee tried to steady his breathing as he listened intently to the two men.

"So what's the story with the guy who owns this place then?" the whistling man asked.

"I don't know." Lee detected a lot of bass in his voice. "He disappeared off the scene, I never knew him. I never met him."

"How did he get your number?" The man with the English accent had an almost whiny tone to his voice.

"I don't know."

"Why threaten you? What did he have to hide?"

"I'm not sure," the foreigner answered.

"You were digging up his garden right?" Lee suddenly became very aware and fretful of the conversation going on in front of him.

"Yes, I figured it would be a good way to bond and I didn't care that it wasn't my garden. I guessed that we'd have done the deal and left the country before the owner came back. If he ever came back at all."

Lee was now confident that the voice was Riso.

"But he *did* come back, a little too early perhaps."

"Exactly, so we rushed things a little bit. Zala is living with that little freak now so we're going to be okay. The con is still on."

Lee's heart stopped beating, he was sure of it. His whole body took a bullet of shock. Astonishment, depression, anger, and hopelessness all sparked inside of him at once.

"How can you let your wife live with another man? Especially a murderer?" the whiny man quizzed.

"I don't think he actually killed his wife, and Zala says he probably didn't do it."

"Either way . . . "

"I trust her," Riso's voice was strong and assertive. "She knows the game."

"Fair enough."

Lee pushed his face back into the fluffy carpet. His heart hadn't stopped beating, but it was beating so fast that the beats seemed to fuse into a constant throb.

"I wonder if he has something to hide." The conversation continued above him with the unknown man asking questions. "What if there's something in the garden? You said you left the bottom part untouched right?"

"Yes," Riso's reply was somewhat impatient.

"What if he was watching you? Maybe he knew you were living here all along and got a fright when you started to dig up his garden."

"I don't know and I don't care, and he's not the reason we're here."

"But still, think about it. Why would he threaten you? Why would he ask you to leave and not just phone the police and get you done for squatting or breaking and entering?"

"There's something going on, but that's none of our business. I don't care about him. I have more important things to deal with."

"His problem could be a big one. I've heard what happens in quiet little pieces of suburbia like this . . . they're all fucking criminals."

"I don't care."

"But—"

"Just get the clothes and let's get out of here," Riso instructed in an impatient and somewhat aggressive tone that Lee had never heard from him before. "We still have all the furniture downstairs."

"You sure this Lee guy will be asleep? This could take a while."

"He'll be fine. Zala knows we're coming tonight, she'll take care of it."

"We're a few hours late."

"It doesn't matter."

"So how much do you think we'll get out of him?"

Lee heard Riso sigh. "I'm still not too happy that you're going to get *anything* out of this. This was mine and Zala's job. I only called you in to help me clear the house."

"And now that I'm in on it, I get a cut. So what's the deal? Is Zala going to actually marry him?"

"No," Riso said abruptly. "There's no need. He has no family or friends. We just need to make sure he has a will."

"Then he pens in Zala, she kills him, makes it look like suicide and *bam*, we're a few million bucks richer, right?"

"Something like that."

"So, is she going to fuck him then?" the English man joked.

"No." Riso's reply was hasty and agitated.

"Why not? It might help speed things along. Hell, if he's that lonely, he might just hand her everything he has as soon as she sucks his cock."

A moment of pained silence broke the conversation before Riso spoke. "Stop talking and start working."

Within minutes, they had stripped the bedroom and gone downstairs.

21

Lee waited underneath the bed in the darkness of the Lechnens' master bedroom, a stale carpet odor flooding his nostrils and lungs. He listened intently to the two men who had just finished removing the couch from the living room, escorting it out of the door and into the van with minimal effort.

Riso wasn't dead. His death was a hoax, a small part of a big hustle. Zala, who had shed fake tears throughout the day and who Lee had comforted with genuine sympathy, was after his money and nothing else.

The pieces of the puzzle began to fit together as he inhaled the dry carpet fibers and listened to the hushed commotion downstairs. The strange glances the couple had exchanged; the phone call Lee had overheard; the missing car; the forward, friendly nature.

Everything clicked seamlessly into place, each piece another knife through Lee's heart. He had trusted both Riso and Zala—he adored Zala and changed his life for her. It was obvious that she liked him: the glances, the laughter, the conversations, the stares, the admiration, and the exchange of personal memories all pointed to an infatuation and that had been enough to keep Lee's mind on the right track. But her flirtatious attitude was nothing more than a show, a committed lie to please him and trick him out of his wealth. He doubted that anything she had told him about her past was real. She probably made everything up just to get close to him, sharing her fake secrets and troubled past in hope that he would share his own.

His anger came in waves, rushing through his blood like a shot of heroin. He wanted to climb out from underneath the bed and attack Riso. His blood boiled when he considered what he had done and he wanted to seek immediate revenge. But he had enough logic left to stop himself from doing that, even in the face of his overwhelming anger.

He continued to toy with the idea of running. The two men were now at the front of the house but soon they would start shifting furniture around the back, taking it through the kitchen and dining room. He knew he could escape. They wouldn't be able to hear his footsteps on the stairs and he would have enough time to run out the door and out of sight before they returned to the van.

When the two men finally did make their way to the kitchen, their heavy boots sending vibrations throughout the house and allowing Lee to pinpoint their positions, he simply sunk his head into the carpet, defeated.

Part of him wanted to get out of there as fast and as soon as possible, another part of him wanted to stay, to wallow in self-pity for a while and wait for the two men to leave before he made his move. Before he could make his up mind, voices from downstairs made it up for him.

"The van is full," stated the man with the English accent, his voice coming between heavy breaths.

"We still have a few more things."

"You should have brought a bigger van."

"It's *your* van."

Their voices became clearer the longer Lee listened, as if his ears were testing the connection and fine tuning after each syllable.

"You could have borrowed one. My mate, well, a friend of a friend, has a *real* transport company, and we could have asked him."

"That's too many people. I didn't even want to get you involved in this," Riso stated firmly.

"Hey!" The man seemed insulted. "I've been your friend for fucking years. We've been to hell and back. I've done over a dozen jobs with you, for fuck's sake."

"I know, I'm sorry, I didn't mean it like that. This was just for me and Zala. That's all I meant."

"Fair enough," his friend agreed. "But now I'm involved, so what are we going to do? Do you want to drive the van back to the garage and drop some of this gear off?"

"It's getting late."

"It's two in the morning, it couldn't get any earlier."

"You know what I mean. We need to clear out before the sun comes up."

"It's twenty minutes to the garage and back," assured the relaxed friend. "Plus ten minutes to clear out the van and another twenty to fill it up again and clear off. We'll have plenty of time to spare." He spoke with greater confidence than Riso, and was clearly less agitated.

"Okay," Riso said unsurely. "Let's go."

Lee listened intently as the couple thudded through the house and left via the front door, closing it silently behind them. He waited a few seconds, listening to the noises of the house and making sure the men didn't decide to make a quick return. He then rolled out from underneath the bed and jumped to his feet.

He watched through the window as the doors to the van gently clicked shut. The driver started the engine, took one quick glance at Lee's house, and drove the van out of the street.

Lee stood at the window with his hands on his hips. Through the expansive studio windows opposite, clouded in darkness and glistening with the reflections of the streetlights, he thought he saw a light momentarily flicker on and off.

He sagged his head to his chest, looked around. The bedroom had been completely stripped. Only the bed and the mattress remained. The cupboards had been thrown open and deprived of their contents, several empty coat-hangers dangled freely.

He quickly turned and ran across the hallway, down the stairs, and out into the fresh air. He didn't stop running until he came to his own doorway. The cool night had turned bitter, the once rejuvenating wind now aggressively attacking the world, tearing at trees, lifting litter into the skies, and flapping at Lee's clothes as he entered his house. This time he wasn't careful or quiet, showing none of the finesse he had displayed upon leaving.

He immediately walked into the living room and plonked himself onto the sofa, flustered. Running his hands across his face, sucking the cold from his cheeks to the palms of his hands, he dropped his head back.

Before he could contemplate his next move, the lights inside the living room exploded into life and a sly, sinister voice spoke to him.

"Where have you been?"

22

Zala Lechnen stood in the doorway leading into the living room, her hands folded across her chest, her fingers gently drumming on her forearms. She was still wearing Lee's shirt, but had covered her slender legs with the body-hugging pair of jeans she had been wearing during the day.

Lee jumped when he heard her voice. Quickly turning toward her, he greeted her with a wide-eyed stare. "Zala," he said softly, his words seemed to fall out of his mouth. "I . . . I went for a walk," he stuttered, struggling to fabricate a lie with his breathless words.

"You seem tired," Zala said with a frosty edge. "Have you been running?"

Lee tried to settle his breathing and calm his nerves. He replied with as much placidity as he could muster. "The wind started to get a bit out of control." He faked a smile as he struggled to retain eye contact. "I jogged half the way back; the cold practically sucked the air out of my lungs." He made a choking sound and followed it with a laugh. "I also freaked out a little in the dark, thought someone was following me. It turned out to be a cat."

"Couldn't you sleep?" Zala said, seemingly warming to his lies.

Lee faked a serious expression and lowered his head. "I started to think about Riso," he began, faking enough empathy to seem genuine. "I guess I was so busy thinking about you all day, making sure you were okay and what not. He was your husband, after all, and I know the pain of losing a spouse . . . " He sighed softly, his head still lowered. "I was so wrapped up with you, I never really thought about how Riso's death affected me. I mean, I didn't know him for very long but still . . . besides you, he was my only friend."

Zala's coldness ceased. "He was a good man, a good husband, and a good friend."

Lee nodded, relieved but still worried. "What are you doing up?"

Zala hesitated before answering. "I was thirsty." She looked toward the kitchen. "I guess all that crying dried me out."

"Why don't you go back to bed and I'll bring you a cup of hot chocolate?"

"No, it's okay," Zala refused, much to his disappointment and frustration. He didn't know what to do, but he did know that he wanted Zala out of the room. She had turned from a beautiful goddess to an evil seductress and he no longer felt comfortable around her.

"Why don't you go put the kettle on?" the succubus said with a smile. "We can watch a bit of television while we have our hot chocolate."

Lee nodded, thought about countering her words, and then headed for the kitchen, defeated. He noticed his hands were trembling when he retrieved two cups from the cupboard. Hearing Zala approach from the rear, he quickly hid his hands in his pockets and turned toward her.

"You should be sleeping," he said, wishing he had stocked something in his cupboards that he could slip into her chocolate.

Zala stared at him, her eyes boring deep into his. "I'm not really that tired," she said blankly. She walked around the kitchen counter and leaned on it, her attention never diverting from him.

Lee coughed awkwardly, clearing his rapidly drying throat. "You've had a long day."

"I'm okay, really."

Lee nodded bleakly. He turned his back to Zala and scooped teaspoons of hot chocolate mix into the empty cups. He stopped what he was doing when a beeping noise alerted him. He looked instantly at Zala.

The hustler seemed embarrassed as she stuck her hand into her pocket and pulled out a mobile phone. "Sorry," she apologized, red-faced. Lee watched her as she jabbed away at the device for several seconds, deep in concentration, before stuffing it back into her pocket. "The battery is dying," she explained in a dry tone.

Lee opened his mouth, ready to quiz her, but he quickly changed his question. "Do you want sugar?"

"No, I'm sweet enough."

The words *lying bitch* quickly entered Joseph's mind. "You certainly are." He scooped three spoonfuls of sugar into his own mug, piling the crystal grains on top of the thick cocoa powder. He figured he would need as much energy as he could get.

A pungent hostility hung in the air. Lee sensed it, he knew it was there, he knew that their conversation was a façade, but he couldn't be certain that Zala knew. Maybe the hostility was all in his mind, a product of the atrocities he had discovered.

When the kettle boiled, he slowly poured hot water into the cups. He could feel the deep, penetrating eyes of Zala Lechnen on him the whole time, as though she was waiting for him to make a move but wasn't sure what his move would be. Lee wasn't sure either; he didn't know whether to run, fight, or talk. He thought about telling her, confronting her and exposing her, but he wasn't living in a romance film; Zala wasn't likely to admit her wrongdoings, apologize, and walk out of his life. She was a criminal and so was her husband. Lee didn't know how dangerous they were or how dangerous they could be when their feathers were ruffled.

He decided that running would not only be cowardly, but would be an incredibly stupid thing to do. He couldn't drive and didn't know the streets. He didn't have a safe place to go to and he cringed at the thought of running to the police. They knew who he was and would probably laugh at him. At best they would send someone to investigate, by which time the Lechnens would be long gone and local law enforcement would have more reason to despise and distrust him.

He didn't want to fight, either. Zala was a slight, slender woman; he cringed at the thought of laying a hand on her, despite the heartbreak she had planned for him. What worried him most weren't the thoughts of fighting, running, or talking, but his delusions of lust and love for her, which still remained, albeit to a lesser degree. A part of him hoped Zala would show some sympathy toward him, that she would acknowledge the time they had spent together, the warmth they had shared and the conversations they had enjoyed. That part of his brain concluded that if he told Zala everything, she would take his side, exposing her love for him and rejecting her undead husband.

He forced those thoughts away, treating them like a disease. He finished filling the cups and handed one of them to Zala, a fake smile on his face.

This wasn't a film—this was real life and Zala was a real criminal. Sweet faced or not, Lee didn't doubt that she would rip him apart to get at his money. There was no chance he could turn her like a romantic twist in a Hollywood thriller. She had started a war and Lee needed to make sure he was on the winning side.

Taking a sip of the hot liquid, he glanced at her through the cloud of thick steam rising from the cup. "Let's go watch some television."

She nodded and motioned for Lee to go into the living room before her.

"After you." He was closer to the door, but he remained where he stood. He wafted his hand as she strode in front of him and headed out of the kitchen. He grimaced at the back of her head, piercing through her skull with a razor-sharp stare. "Ladies first," he said quietly.

———

They sat next to each other on the sofa. His mind was rife with thoughts, so much so that he couldn't concentrate on what he was doing. Without realizing it, he tuned into a channel broadcasting a blue screen and the message that programs would commence at 8:00 a.m. He then put the remote down and settled back, gripping the mug of hot chocolate like someone stranded in the desert would hold his only bottle of water.

Zala looked at him, baffled, her gaze flickered from the television to his face. "Are you enjoying this?" she wondered.

"Hmm?" Lee had tried to become so alert to Zala's actions that he had almost forgot to listen to her words.

"Change the channel, for God's sake," she said with a laugh, nudging him.

He watched the hot chocolate swirl around in the mug, reacting to the light shove. He picked up the remote again and aimlessly switched channels. He stopped when he saw what appeared to be an action movie.

It soon became apparent—after a scene of a Japanese sword wielding maniac switched to a romantic scene plucked from a teen comedy—that the channel was just running a series of movie trailers.

"Here!" Zala shot her hand across Lee's body, reaching for the remote. He flinched at her sudden movement but she didn't seem to notice. "Give it to me, I'll find something."

Lee handed her the remote, not making eye contact.

"You're useless." She grinned at him.

She quickly found what appeared to be a drama series. Lee watched intently, but his eyes saw past the screen, into his own thoughts. Zala yawned heavily, cupping her hand over her mouth. She curled her legs up on the sofa, shifted them underneath her backside, and then leaned into Lee, resting her head on his shoulders.

He looked down at the top of her head in disgust. He had loved it when she cuddled into him. He had cherished every moment he had spent in close contact with her, admiring her warmth and her fragrance. Now he resented it. He felt awkward and uncomfortable with her resting on him, like being hugged by a sweaty stranger in a nightclub or kissed by a ninety-year-old aunt he hadn't seen since childhood.

Zala seemed to pick up on this. She lifted her head to speak, her face inches from his. "Are you okay?"

"I'm fine," he lied. He felt his body shudder involuntary. He tried to disguise it by following it with a stretch and a yawn. "I think I'm just tired."

"You feel uncomfortable." She prodded his shoulder.

"Maybe I should put on some weight, give you a decent cushion to lie on," he joked.

"I didn't mean like that," she replied with a giggle, a sound that angered and agitated Lee's blood now that he knew it was an act. "Never mind," she conceded. "Just stay still." She rested her head on his shoulder and Lee stiffened.

For ten minutes, they watched television in silence. He never removed his eyes from the screen but he had no idea what he had seen. He wasn't entirely sure what was on. He made a move, leaning away from Zala, who immediately lifted her head. He placed his empty cup on the floor, slapped his hands on his thighs in dramatic fashion, and then stood.

"Where are you going?" she snapped quickly.

"I'm just going to the toilet," he said softly, somewhat startled at her tone.

"Okay." She feigned a smile and flopped to where Lee had been sitting, settling into the pre-warmed cushions.

When he set foot on the bottom stair, he heard her inquisitive voice call to him, "Why don't you use the one downstairs?"

"There are some pills I need to get in the upstairs bathroom," he said, thinking on his feet. The downstairs toilet was small and within sight of the living room. He felt the urge to get as far away from Zala as possible.

"You're popping pills now?" she joked.

Lee made faces at her through the wall, saluting her with two fingers. "They're just herbal sleep aids," he said lightly.

"If they're any good, leave some for me, would you?"

"Okay," Lee called back pleasantly, cursing under his breath as he climbed the stairs. "*Fucking evil little bitch.*"

His nerves kicked in when he reached the top. His extremities ran cold and his legs trembled. It hit like an unexpected rush of blood—he felt like he had been sitting down for hours and had stood up too fast. His world turned into a blurry concoction of flashing stars, blood thumped through his ears like a bass drum. The fear and reality of the situation grabbed him and pulled him down. Using the banister, he slowly lowered himself to the floor until he was sitting on the top step, his arms still stretched above him, gripping the wooden rail.

Holding his head in his hands, he waited for the dizziness to cease. He was in a mess that he wasn't sure he could break out of, and the more he thought about it, the worse it seemed. He remembered the conversation between Riso and his friend; they had only left to clear the van. Soon they would be back and, if they discovered that Lee had been eavesdropping on them, they wouldn't be happy.

He waited for his vision to clear and found himself recounting Zala's words and trying to read her body language. She had watched him enter the house in a fluster, and his cover story had been weak to say the least, but if she knew he was lying surely she would have ran out of the house, looking for the arms of her lover and accomplice in crime.

He analyzed the thoughts until his head hurt.

He walked to the main bathroom and immediately spun the cold tap before sitting down on the edge of the bath. What had begun as an opportunity to be with a beautiful woman had quickly turned into a sick game in which he was the victim. He was having trouble coming to terms with the change. His dead friend had become a living enemy, the girl of his dreams had jumped into his nightmares, and the only person to trust him after the death of his wife, perhaps the only person who genuinely believed he didn't kill her, was a professional liar. What made matters worse was that the very woman who was causing all of his troubles was waiting for him downstairs. He had become a prisoner in his own home.

He sat on the edge of the bathtub with his head in his hands for what seemed like hours, contemplating what had gone on before and wondering how to resolve the situation. When he finally lifted his head, he stared at a small clock on the wall next to the door. He had been in the bathroom for more than ten minutes and Zala hadn't called for him. He felt the tension in his shoulders dissipate, the weight hanging from the back of his mind lighten. Maybe she had run away, he wondered with delight. Maybe, just like him, she had been waiting for the ideal time to flee, running out of the house and out of his life when he went upstairs.

Confident tricksters were not violent. When trouble arose, they either talked their way out of it or they ran. By going upstairs, Lee had given her the perfect opportunity to flee. She could find her lover, leave the area, and count their losses.

Ice-cold water rushed from the tap, splashing around the sink. He scooped up handfuls and splashed it on his face, bringing some life back into his tired features. He stared at himself in the mirror above the sink. A circle of red had formed around his left pupil—a deep scarlet pool of blood enveloped the tiny orb. Black bags hung underneath his eyes in burrowed pits. His lips were cracked and dried, sporting spots of black, red, and flaky pink where the skin had begun to peel.

He examined his lips like a child would examine a scab, picking to discover bits that wouldn't be painful to remove before violently detaching them with a pinched finger and a quick pull. He wiped his face and checked his appearance before leaving the bathroom.

At the top of the stairs he waited, sucking in deep breaths to calm himself and keep his heart from exploding out of his chest. He could hear sounds from the television but nothing else. Steadying himself with a succession of deep breaths and a multitude of mental warm-ups, he began his descent.

He let his head hang as he stepped off the stairs and into the hallway, his eyes passing over the spot on the floor that had haunted him for nearly a year. He lifted his gaze as he walked through the open doorway into the living room.

Zala was nowhere to be seen but Lee was petrified by what he saw. Fear hit his heart like a knife and every muscle in his body tensed.

"Hello, Mr. Lee."

Joseph could only stare blankly, his body frozen.

Riso Lechnen stood in the center of the living room, his tall and strong posture dominating the room. His arms were folded across his huge chest. His eyes showed a glint of sadism as he stared.

"What's wrong?" he asked softly. "Not expecting me?"

23

Joseph Lee stared in disbelief at the "dead man" standing in front of him. He took a step forward, breaking the freeze that had engulfed his body, the ice cracking in his stiff muscles. He began to ask a question, but he wasn't given the chance.

Something struck him from behind, a solid blunt object smacking against the back of his knees. He lost control of his legs. They crumpled as though they weren't his own. The shocked face of Riso Lechnen flashed out of his vision as he dropped, sounding screams of anguish.

Blinking through the pain, he saw something flash across his gaze as the rounded end of a wooden bat flew toward him. He didn't have time to react and merely closed his eyes in preparation.

Initially, he felt the bat clip the top of his skull, and an explosion of pain, beginning at the base, rocked through his brain. This was quickly followed by a second round of pain, a delayed crushing agony that alerted every nerve in his body, flushing them with torment. His body drunkenly rocked to the side but didn't roll over. Sitting back on his heels, he clasped his head in his arms and assumed the fetal position.

"What the fuck are you doing!" someone screamed above him. Their voice was distant and flat, as if filtered through a wall.

"Drop that!" someone else shouted from further across the room.

Lee opened his eyes to stare at his own knees. His pupils wobbled, his vision was blurred and shaky. He tipped his forehead to rest on his knee, his head feeling heavy.

"What?" This voice came from behind him, close enough to make his aching body shudder. "He's fine," it said casually.

Suppressing the urge to vomit, Lee rolled his head to one side. A wound at the back of his head was dripping blood—strained through his own hair—along the side of his face and off his forehead, landing in a small pool to the right of his knees. The spinning room, the stabbing pain, and the sight of his own blood turned his stomach.

"Why did you bring that fucking thing?" a voice, like an echo, sounded across the room.

"I *had* to bring him."

"Ha ha, very fucking funny." The voice from behind him unsettled his nerves and he inadvertently twitched to one side. The attacker had been hiding against the wall next to the door, waiting for Lee to appear before mercilessly battering him.

"*The bat*. Why did you bring the bat?"

The fibers from the carpet brushed the side of his head. The blood trickled away from his forehead, around the back of his head, dripping onto the cream carpet. A ring of crimson stained his forehead like a morbid halo.

"In case there was any trouble." He recognized the voice as the man who had helped Riso empty his house.

Fighting against his own instinct—which wanted to curl up and die—Lee used the anger inside of him to force his eyes and mind into focus, pushing the pain away.

Resting on the floor, lying on his left cheek, he surveyed the room. The big, intimidating stature of Riso Lechnen stood just in front of him, his attention aimed past Lee and at the man who had ambushed him. His huge feet and thick leather boots were in reach, as were his bulging calves.

"Why did you swing? He didn't move."

Lee shifted his eyes away from Riso and concentrated on the far end of the living room. Standing near the entrance to the kitchen, some distance from the action, was the once angelic figure of Zala Lechnen. She expressed anger at her incompetent and trigger-happy accomplice, but she seemed to show little regard for Lee's predicament.

"Does it matter?"

"You could have killed him!" Zala said angrily.

"Why should *you* care? Have you and him got something going on?"

"Fuck you," Zala snapped. "If you kill him, you kill our chance of getting any money."

"That's the only reason? Are you *sure* you didn't fuck him?" he teased.

"Bastard!" Zala spat aggressively. She stormed across the room toward Lee and the maniac behind him. Riso also moved. Sensing his wife's aggression, he turned away from Lee to focus his attention on her.

Joseph acted as quickly as his aching body would allow. Fear and adrenaline took control. He shot out an arm and grabbed Riso's exposed shin. Kicking off the floor for leverage, he flipped his wrist and pulled his arm backward, yanking Riso's foot out from underneath him.

The big man was taken unaware and instantly lost mobility. He stumbled. Before anyone else in the room could act or think, Lee sprang to his feet—ignoring a rush of pain that shot through his skull—and rounded the Austrian, wrapping his left forearm around his neck. He struggled with him, upper-body strength fighting upper-body strength as he tried to pull Riso's neck back to fully shield his own body and complete the vice-like headlock.

He hadn't thought about what to do next—trying to wrestle a man taller than him and twice his weight had been enough to worry about—but the bat-wielding accomplice canceled the need for thought.

He quickly swung the bat with all his might, aiming for Lee's head and threatening to take it off. Lee managed to momentarily win the struggle. He yanked Riso's head up in front of his own.

Riso, noticing the presence of the bat, twisted his face in horror. He tried to squirm away but his actions were feeble. The face of the man wielding the bat also changed as he realized the inevitable problem but was powerless to stop it — the bat already in full swing.

Lee ducked backward as wood met flesh and bone. The bat crashed against Riso's skull, cracking it like an egg. A shower of blood sprayed in a 360-degree shower of carnage, covering Lee's face and the living room in the thick crimson fluid.

A blood-curdling squeal of horror sounded from across the room before everything turned eerily quiet.

Riso's body became limp and lifeless and Lee struggled to hold onto the heavy weight. The Austrian's chin hung from his forearm, his head arched backward into Lee's chest, his lower body crumpled to the floor. Lee looked down, staring straight into lifeless eyes. Blood seeped through a gaping wound in Riso's head and soaked straight into Lee's torso.

Lee released his grip and watched the body drop like a rag doll, twisting lifelessly in on itself. From across the room, Zala had watched the spectacle in horror. She tried to run to her husband's aide but her legs gave out and she fell to her trembling knees.

Lee watched her cry; a violent, horrible emotion. Her whole body shook, tears gushing from her reddened eyes. He had seen her cry before but none of her previous tears had been real. She roared and moaned, noises spilled out from her mouth randomly and incoherently. She reached out her arms, trying to touch her husband, who lay dead eight feet away from her.

Lee was so distracted by Zala's tears, he didn't see the butt of the baseball bat rushing toward him. It hit him on his nose, the rubber handle flattening and crushing the appendage. A violent flow of blood, which he caught with his hands, gushed out from his nose as he stumbled backward.

The attacker dropped the bat and advanced on Lee with a fearless look of hatred in his eyes. He swung his right hand and made clean contact with Joseph's face. His fist smacked Lee's hand, covering his bleeding nose, and forced it back into his face.

He then jabbed with his left, his knuckles clattering Lee's ear and sending him stumbling sideways, just in time to receive another right hook that swept across Lee's face, skimming his cheek, nose, and lips.

With hands covered in blood that wasn't his own, and with his former friend and colleague lying dead by his feet, the man continued to punch. A left hook below Lee's ribs sucked the air out of his lungs and forced him to double over. A heavy punch fell down on top of his head, pushing Lee down further. The attacker then delivered a blow with his knee.

The blow sucked all the fire out of Joseph and replaced it with burning agony. He fell to the floor on his hands and knees, gasping for breath as blood poured over his face. He coughed violently as the fluid dripped into his mouth. Saliva-fused crimson dripped from his chin like thick soup.

"You killed him!" Zala was screaming. "You killed Riso!" She pounded the floor with her fists.

"It was an accident!" the man explained to the grieving widow. "Get over it and get on your feet!"

"*Get over it*? My husband is fucking dead!"

Lee lifted his head and smiled, blood had stuck to his teeth. "Get over it, Zala," he coughed. "It's not the first time, is it?" he laughed painfully.

A leather boot wrapped around his head and sent him spinning across the floor.

"Fuck!" he coughed, spitting a glob of blood on the carpet.

"Watch your fucking mouth!" the murderer ordered.

"What do you want?" Lee rasped.

"Your money asshole, what do you think?"

"And you think this is the way to go about getting it?" Lee wanted to know. His adrenaline kicked back in. He lifted to a seated position and stared at the murderer.

"Shut the fuck up and don't move!" the murderer ordered. He turned to Zala. "Does he have a safe or something?"

"No!" she spat. "This isn't a fucking robbery. Do you know *anything*?"

"Riso said this guy was loaded."

"He is."

"So where is his money?"

"In the bank!" Zala screamed aggressively. Grief and anger had fueled together inside her and the collage of emotion was aimed at the unknown assailant. "You've fucked this up!" she accused. "I don't know why Riso asked you in on this but—"

"He needed my help," the man argued. He had taken a few steps closer to Zala. "Without me, we wouldn't *be* here."

"Exactly!"

"Look, you needed me to clear out the house. It wasn't my fault Riso died," he replied casually, showing little remorse.

"*You* were the one who fucking killed him!"

Lee edged closer to the door during the commotion. He inched past the couch, out of view of Zala, who would see him if he shifted any further. He peeped around the couch and watched her arguing as she kneeled on the floor. Saliva dripped down her chin and shot out of her mouth as she spoke. She resembled an angry dog.

"I didn't *mean* to kill him."

"Oh, well that's okay then."

Lee looked to the doorway. He calculated five steps between him and the exit, five steps that would be seen by Zala. Then another six or seven steps to the front door. If he moved quickly enough and didn't waste time opening the door, he could be out of the house just as Riso's killer had worked out what was going on and long before Zala could jump to her feet.

"I'm sorry, okay?"

"No, it's *not* fucking okay!" Zala growled. "You killed my husband. You're a fucking incompetent freak!" she barked.

Lee made his move. He kicked off the floor like a sprinter from the blocks, moving low and with a great burst of speed. He reached the front door in a second. As his right hand felt the cold metal of the handle, he heard Zala call out behind him "*. . . stop him!*"

He pulled open the door, burst out into the night, and gave the door a quick flick with his wrist so that it swung closed behind him.

His feet wobbled as he ran, his legs shaky and weak. His world was still hazy, his body still in agony, but a shot of adrenaline urged him to continue. A cold wind rushed at his face and dried the dripping blood as he pushed on past the pain barrier. His breaths were short and harsh, every movement took a great deal of exertion but he continued running for his life.

At the end of the driveway, he turned left out of his property and down the footpath.

He then stopped dead in his tracks. His thighs and quads burned from the sudden jolt, his kneecap made a sharp and painful shift. A silver pistol, fitted with a black silencer, was held by steady hands and aimed directly at his face. The cold barrel was inches from his flesh.

He grumbled breathlessly, his eyes on the barrel.

The Lechnens' accomplice sprinted down the driveway, desperately trying to catch up with Lee. He skidded around the corner and stopped just behind him, seemingly as surprised as Lee had been.

"Hello, Joseph," the figure holding the gun spoke from the shadows. "And I see you have a friend." He waved the gun at the man behind him. "Both of you get back inside, now!" he ordered.

24

Lee followed Riso's killer back into the house with the armed man trailing close behind. They met with Zala who had dragged herself to her feet to wait near the front door. She raised her arms above her head when she saw the gun. In the short silence, her eyes quickly darted around, studying Lee and then Riso's friend, hoping to grasp an understanding of what had happened. As the men approached, she took a few steps away from the doorway, allowing them inside.

Lee entered the house as Zala and her accomplice lined up in front of the stairs. He heard the door slam shut behind him. The wind helped it close with an angry gust and it rattled in its frame, sending a shockwave of vibrations through the floor.

In the light of the house, he studied the man wielding the gun. He was disheveled and bedraggled. He wore all black: loose-fitting black trousers, dusty black shoes, and a black T-shirt underneath a black jacket. He even wore a black baseball cap. His skin was pale and sickly. His face was rough; his gray eyes were baggy and tired. The menacing orbs studied their surroundings with quick fleeting glances and seemed to glow with a manic ferocity when they met with another gaze.

Stubble pricked through his skin and covered his chin and cheeks. He looked no older than forty and already the hairs on his face were beginning to match the color of his skin. His hair glittered with silver strands.

"Who are you?" The question had been on Lee's lips, but it was the man in black who asked it, his gun aimed at the Lechnens' accomplice.

"I should be asking you the same question," the casual criminal replied cockily, apparently unaware of any danger.

"I'm the one with the gun," the newcomer reminded him sternly.

"Fair enough. I'm . . . " he paused, shooting a look at Lee.

"Yes?"

"I'm nobody," he said, smiling lightly.

The gunman nodded. "Good," he said in a placid tone, nodding and smiling before unceremoniously squeezing the trigger. The suppressor sucked some of the noise out of the shot, but the lethal device still thundered, shaking the house and causing Lee to grasp at his ears.

The cocky accomplice, who had delivered the fatal blow to his partner in crime, dropped straight to the floor. His legs folded inward, his backside resting upon his heels. His lifeless face looked toward the ceiling, his dead eyes toward the heavens. A fresh bullet hole above his right eye leaked a steady stream of blood over his face, coloring his features.

Zala sobbed a muffled scream as she saw the man crumple to his knees out of the corner of her eyes. She didn't dare turn to look. She stared at the gunman, watching as he aimed the gun at her.

"And you?" he asked, a sickeningly sadistic smile on his face. His deluded eyes seemed to sparkle, reveling in her fear.

"Zala, Zala Lechnen," she quickly answered, clearing her throat.

"Good." He paused, watching the fear in Zala's eyes as he steadied the gun's aim around her face. He waited until fear ran uncontrollably through her body, forcing her into more tears. She closed her eyes and waited for him to pull the trigger.

Grinning, he shifted the gun to Lee. "Hello again," he said.

"Do we know each other?" Lee tried his best to maintain eye contact.

"Not really. I'm a friend of a friend, so to speak."

"I don't have any friends."

"You *did*." He grinned and then waved the gun toward the living room. "Get in there," he ordered. "Sit down."

Zala sat next to Lee on the sofa. They exchanged brief and awkward glances but didn't utter a word. The gunman wandered around the room, fascinated with the scenes of carnage. Lee and Zala sat in silence, too afraid to move. Not only was the stranger carrying a loaded gun, but he seemed to have no quarrels about using it.

After a few seconds, the pale-faced maniac returned with the baseball bat that had killed Riso and injured Lee. He handed it to Lee. "Hold this."

Lee obeyed and grabbed the bat by the handle. The gunman pushed it up and down, rubbing the entire handle of the bat against Lee's willing hands.

"Thank you," he said politely, removing it from Lee's grasp. He produced a handkerchief from his jacket pocket and wiped away his fingerprints from the parts of the bat he had touched before tossing it to the floor, where it bounced off Riso's corpse and landed on the soft carpet.

A breath escaped Riso's dead lungs as the bat bounced off his chest, almost unnoticed by the two men but not by Zala. The fear and tension in her body was now so intense, she began to twitch and shudder uncontrollably.

"What's going on?" Lee wanted to know. He felt increasingly awkward, angry, and pitiful sitting next to Zala. He could feel her presence and her heat. He also felt the suppressed sobs and violent shudders that rocked her body. He knew he couldn't rely on her for a joint escape effort—fear had paralyzed her and loss had made her passive.

The gunman walked around the sofa and stood in front of the television, demanding attention from both his subjects. His eyes were fixed lustfully on Zala, but he spoke to Lee. "I've been to this house before," he declared.

"Who are you?" Lee demanded to know.

He dragged his eyes away from Zala and focused a sly smile at Lee. "Patrick Rose," he said genuinely, reaching out his free hand for Lee to shake.

Lee accepted the gesture and reached to meet the hand.

"Fuck off." The gunman quickly withdrew. "As if," he laughed immaturely.

"What do you want?" Lee begged.

"I could name a few things," Patrick said lustfully, his eyes bearing a hole through Zala as he licked his lips.

"Fuck you!" Zala tried to break her passivity, her words harsh but her tone soft.

"Maybe later, darling." He blew her a kiss. "First we have some business to attend to." He turned back to Lee. "You," he pointed aggressively with the gun, "you killed your wife a year ago and then—"

Lee sighed, "No, no, no," he shook his head. "That's why you're here? You're one of *them*? Don't you think this is a little extreme?" he barked with frustration and disbelief.

"What are you talking about, *piss-stain*?" the gunman spat the insult like a carefree teenager.

"You think I killed my wife so—"

"Correction," Patrick interrupted. "I *know* you *didn't* kill your wife. I know for a fact," he stated with a sure nod.

Lee nodded, thinking he was dealing with a deluded pervert. "Oh, in that case, where were you a year ago when I needed you?" he asked sarcastically.

"I was killing your wife," Patrick replied plainly, smiling as he watched Lee's jaw drop.

"*You?*"

"Yes, me," he said proudly. "Only I didn't really—"

"Why?" Where there should have been anger, Lee could only feel awakening remorse and bewilderment.

"Because I loved her," Patrick replied bluntly, with a smile that suggested a lot more.

Lee's eyebrows raised in confusion.

"I was fucking her behind your back." Patrick laughed. "She had many 'late nights at the office' at my house. Every night for a year, I pounded that sweet pussy." He flashed a sickly grin that angered Lee.

"You're lying," Lee accused, hoping he was.

"God's honest truth." He held his hand to his heart and laughed.

"But . . . why . . . " Lee was at a loss for words. He'd spent many sleepless nights thinking about meeting Jennifer's killer. Not only did he want to tear him limb from limb but he had so many questions. He struggled to recall any.

Patrick merely shook his head. "They were the best months of my life, such a tight ass." His eyes flickered as he remembered. "It was a shame really."

"Why?" Lee felt his body tear in two, half of him screamed in anger, the other half sat back in frozen disbelief. Sorrow sided with both halves.

"It's a long story."

"We have all night," Zala chimed in.

Patrick looked at the Austrian with shock at first, but his features gradually converted back to their lustful roots. "Okay, little lady," he said, "just for you. If you must know . . . " he took a few steps back, until he was leaning against the back wall.

"I was married when I first started seeing her. At first it was only once a week, if that—it was just a sexual thing. I don't think she was too happy at home, she either wasn't getting any or what she *was* getting wasn't any good." He glanced at Lee, waiting for retaliation, but Lee was still in shock. "Things started to get more intense. My wife started to work away so I made sure I worked at home." He winked at Lee but he was still unresponsive.

"Eventually we were seeing each other every day. Then my wife lost her job." He shifted his position on the wall. "She was home all the time, complaining, nagging . . . " A scowl crossed his face as he recalled. "I hated that fucking bitch."

He took a deep breath before continuing, "One night, she caught me and Jennifer at it. She was supposed to be at her sister's house but . . . well, she wasn't. Jennifer watched me argue with her, she couldn't help it. My wife dragged her into it. Before we knew what was going on, my wife had gone fucking bonkers and grabbed a knife. She chased me around the bedroom. She nearly fucking killed me but Jennifer came to my aide. She knocked her out with a golfing trophy . . . " His evil eyes shone and he tapped the barrel of the pistol against his skull. "Or at least she *thought* she'd knocked her out."

Lee looked deep into the gunman's eyes.

"You see, Joseph," Patrick said. "*Your* wife killed *my* wife."

"No," Lee denied softly.

"Yes." Patrick laughed. "Don't get me wrong—I'm fucking glad she did—but it did cause some problems. Together we buried the body in the back garden, and that would have been the end of that if Jennifer hadn't had a crisis of fucking conscience." He threw his hands up in the air. "She told me she wanted to go to the police. She said she'd take all the blame, blah blah blah. The fact was: I couldn't let her do that. I was as involved as she was. I dug the grave, for fuck's sake. I couldn't allow Jennifer to give us up."

"So you killed her?" Zala quizzed.

Patrick nodded. "But I made a few mistakes. You," he looked at Lee, "should have been implemented in the murder. You should have been locked up. I was in the process of setting you up when I heard you getting out of the shower."

"You tried to set me up?"

"Tried and failed, but everyone deserves a second chance, don't they?"

"You bastard," Lee leapt up from the sofa and charged at the gunman like a raging bull. The man in black anticipated the attack, stepped to the side, and rammed the butt of the pistol across his face. The metal crunched against his jaw, dislodging two teeth and reverberating through his cheek bones. He dropped to the floor at his attacker's feet.

"Nice try," Patrick said blandly. "You know, you should have never been so trusting of Jennifer. She was a beautiful and sweet girl, with a body that anyone would love to get inside . . . " He retrieved something from the back of his memories that brought a lurid smile to his face. "All those late nights she spent at the office, all those 'neighborhood parties' and 'visits'" he said, making air quotes.

Lee coughed violently and spat at Patrick's feet.

"She hated the neighbors just as much as you. I mean, she spoke to them occasionally. She kept up appearances . . . but nothing more. It was all lies to keep you away. If she said she was going to see them for a coffee and a chat, she knew you'd refuse to tag along." He looked down at Lee and laughed. "She couldn't use work as an excuse all the time, so she used your social hatred against you. Whenever she popped out to borrow a cup of sugar, believe me, she was getting something a lot sweeter."

Lee angrily swung for Patrick's leg, but his attempt was ushered away with a shift kick. Steel-toed boots crushed against his palms and he recoiled.

"I lived across the street from you, for fuck's sake," Patrick continued to gloat. "I was your horny wife's convenient holiday home." He laughed again.

"Fuck you!" Lee screamed. Saliva dripped madly from his mouth, shooting out in torrents as he bellowed angry words. "You *fucking bastard!*"

Patrick merely smiled. He concentrated his attention on Zala, smiling at her at first, as if he had just noticed her from across a crowded room and was trying to make a gentle approach. He then wondered: "So, have you two . . . ?"

"No," Zala answered sharply.

"You're not missing out on much, darling," Patrick assured. "Just ask Jennifer."

Lee spat another glob of blood at the man above him but was quickly pushed back to the floor by the heel of his boot.

"You look a lot like her. I suppose that's the whole point, isn't it? That's why you came here to con him. You hoped that this little unsociable bastard would pay attention to you because you look so much like his dead wife." He paused to look around the room, noting the two dead men. "Clearly, you fucked up."

"It's your fault," Zala said, her tone tired and defeated. "Rose," she said, as if plucking the name from her memory. "It's your house—you were the one who forced us out, you're the reason Riso is dead."

"No." Patrick shook his head slowly. "I didn't kill your husband. His own stupidity did that for him. It's rather ironic that you picked my house to squat in, though, don't you think?"

Lee could hear Zala sigh. "What do you want?" she asked. The knowledge of the assailant's identity seemed to dispel some of her fear.

"I want you two to come with me." He kicked Lee, prodding him in the chest with the tip of his boot. "Get up, prick," he ordered. "We're going across the road to do a little digging."

Lee stumbled out of the house with Zala and Patrick close behind. Patrick, who had taken a liking to Zala, held her by the hand as he ushered her out of the house. Lee wasn't sure whether the man was a sadistic joker who enjoyed toying with Zala or whether he was a maniac who actually wanted to hold her hand and keep her close. Clearly he was a maniac, but to what degree, Lee had yet to discover.

Lee trudged across the street with an apathetic mind. He had always wanted to discover the identity of Jennifer's killer, but everything that had come with learning that identity had taken him somewhere he didn't want to go. Not only was Jennifer having an affair, but she had killed someone. The image of the sweet and innocent woman who had loved him despite everything and would continue to love him had vanished. Inside of him, where there should have been anger or fear, there was only a black hole.

"Hey!" Zala screamed.

"Shut your fucking mouth," Patrick said through gritted teeth. "You'll wake up the fucking neighbors."

"You grabbed my ass."

"You should be happy, you have a nice ass. It was a compliment." He gave her a wink.

Lee found it hard to believe that Jennifer, *his Jennifer*, had found anything worth loving in the sleazy sadist.

"You fucking pervert."

"Now, now . . . calm down. I hate it when we fight."

The three crossed the road and walked down the side of what was, for a short time, the Lechnens' house. They made their way to the back garden where Patrick instructed them to head for the bottom, the part that Lee and Riso had left unfinished.

There were two shovels waiting for them. Lee stopped and waited for Patrick, who was cheekily trying to cuddle an aggressive and agitated Zala.

"Keep your fucking hands off me," she warned.

"I really don't like it when you talk to me like that."

"I don't fucking—"

Patrick drove the butt of the pistol into her face. The metal crushed her nose and sliced through the skin on her cheek. She spun away and clutched her wounds.

"Like I said. I don't like it when you talk like that." He reached forward and pulled her hand away from her face. He studied the marks. "Damn, look what you've made me do. We'll have to get that cleaned up before we do anything." He let her hand drop and turned his attention to Lee.

Zala spoke before he did: "*Do* anything?" she repeated worryingly.

Patrick smiled and gazed into her once twinkling and now horrified eyes, "What did you think I was going to do with you?" His eyes gleamed as he spoke.

"I . . . I . . . " Zala stuttered, "I don't know."

"After we frame this little prick here." He waved the gun at Lee. "You and I are going on a little journey. I have a cabin a few hours from here. Once we get there I'll show you a good time."

"No!" Zala spat, her voice splitting. "I won't let you touch me."

Patrick showed her the gun. "I'm sure I can convince you." He smiled and reached for her face. "You really do look a lot like her," he said softly, sweetly, caressing the skin below her wounds. "I thought I'd never find anybody as sweet as Jen but you . . . you're something else."

Zala slapped his hand away, pushing him away. Patrick laughed, a throaty cackle.

She looked across at Lee, her eyes bore deeply into his. For a second she allowed him to see that she was scared, desperate, and sorry. She wanted his help. He saw a deep-rooted fear in her moist eyes, a desire to be saved.

"You," Patrick attracted Lee's attention, waving the gun around. "Dig," he instructed, aiming the barrel at the ground.

Lee picked up the shovel and stuck it in the mud. Patrick's attention turned back toward Zala. "I wish I could take you inside right now," he said lustfully, almost drooling.

Zala turned away in disgust. As she turned, she caught Lee's gaze and they stared at each other; Zala apologetic, Lee unforgiving.

He made his first cut through the grass and mud.

———

"What exactly is your plan?" Lee wondered, breathlessly. He had only dug five shovelfuls and sweat had already formed on his bloodied forehead.

Throughout his digging, Zala had been watching him, Patrick had been watching Zala, and Lee had fixed his eyes on the ground.

"This is not a *Bond* movie, Mr. Lee," Patrick said simply.

"You have a gun, so you keep reminding us, what am I going to do? Just tell me."

Patrick turned away from Zala and looked suspiciously at Lee, weighing him up. "I'm going to finish something I started years ago."

"What was that?"

"It's simple, really. The police discover the bodies of this little madam's husband." He tilted his head to Zala. "And his friend . . . " He paused and pondered his words momentarily.

"Hmm," he said after much contemplation.

"Hmm?" Joseph wondered.

Patrick shot an aggressive look at Lee. "You fucked up my plan a little bit," he said after a short silence.

"Sorry." Lee almost laughed.

"It's okay," Patrick said, seemingly missing the point. "I'm sure I can work a way around it."

Lee nodded in disbelief as the maniac gently tapped the barrel of the gun to his chin, his mind running through a series of scenarios. Eventually he said, "If you hadn't have killed that big fucker things would have been a lot easier."

"I do apologize."

"I know!" A lightbulb flashed above the psychopath's head. "He was getting too close to discovering your truth: that you killed my wife and buried her in this garden. To shut him up, you killed him, disposing of his pathetic little friend in the crossfire." He seemed satisfied with his conclusion.

"The police arrive and after a bit of digging, so to speak, they find out that you killed my wife, which leads them to the conclusion that you and her were having an affair, ultimately giving you motive to kill Jennifer. They've practically been begging for evidence to lock you away and, once we get your prints all over her, they'll have what they want."

"You expect me to just sit back and let you do that? I don't want to spend the rest of my life in prison." Lee wiped his brow, removing a line of sweat and blood.

"I *don't* and you *won't*. Ah damn, now look what you've done. You've ruined the surprise . . . You see." he grinned sadistically. "I'm going to kill you. Well, technically, *she* will kill you." He motioned to Zala. "Before going on the run. You see, there's something Little Miss Sweet-fuck hasn't told you: she's wanted in three countries. If the police get their hands on her, she'll be spending the next twenty years behind bars." He smiled crudely, lifting a hand to gently stroke Zala's tear-stained cheek. "That would be such a terrible waste."

"So," he concluded, snapping out of whatever lurid fantasy his lustful brain had concocted. "I'll be taking her with me. Just to keep her safe, of course."

Lee didn't react. He remained placid, indifferent. "So why am I digging up your wife?" he wondered.

"Because *I* buried her, there's too much evidence linking me down there. I want you to dig it up and shift that evidence onto you. You'll stick her in the van outside." He looked to Zala. "Your husband was so kind to leave me the keys. Well, they were in his pocket, but I'm sure he won't mind me taking them. I can make it look like Lee got scared and tried to move the body."

Lee nodded and picked up the shovel to continue his work while Patrick lusted over Zala, keeping a safe distance from Lee as he did so.

———

Joseph paused after only a couple of digs, his body aching. His head still throbbed from the earlier blow, as did his legs. The effort of digging exaggerated those pains and created more.

He turned toward Patrick, expecting to be ordered to continue or whipped into action, but the gun-wielding madman was far too interested in Zala. He had forced himself closer to the bereaved Austrian. With the gun in his right hand, aimed at her head, he scooped her in his left arm, dragging her body to his. He whispered things in her ear as she squirmed, her face a picture of disgust.

"Get away from me," she begged, trying to shove him away.

"You like to play hard to get, do you?"

"You're fucking sick," Zala protested. She pushed him backward, swinging wildly with her left arm. Her knuckles struck hard against his temple and he stumbled, just managing to retain his grip on the gun.

Still rocked from the blow, he advanced on Zala with a ferocious lust in his eyes. Zala kicked out. Her pointed boots drilled into Patrick's shins and, with a shocked groan, he almost dropped to his knees. Using his uninjured leg to keep his balance, he rushed upright and pounced on her. He wrapped a hand around her mouth, silenced her screams. He squeezed his palm tight, cutting her lip on her own teeth.

"You shouldn't have done that," he said sternly, bringing his face close to hers.

He drove his knee into her stomach. Instantly her face twisted as the breath was sucked out of her. She tried to scream, but to no avail. He slid his hand away from her mouth, grabbed her hair, and yanked it back with almost enough force to snap her neck.

Zala squealed.

"I think I need to teach you a lesson." He raised his hand above her face, showing her the ominous sight of the gun, her painful fate. "I hope this—"

He finished with a muffled scream.

The blade of a shovel crashed into his fist. A sickening sound of breaking bones and popping knuckles overlapped the agonizing yelp as his hand was smashed to a pulp. The gun flew from his grasp, spinning into the darkness. It landed out of view in the soft muddy ground.

Patrick looked down at his hand, horrified. Two fingers had snapped and pointed backward. His middle finger had bent sideways and rested on the top of his palm. His little finger had been crushed, resting horizontally across his knuckles with the bloodied tip pointing toward his wrist.

"You fucking bastard—"

Joseph swung the shovel again, aiming for the gunman's head. The contact was clean and precise, the metal of the shovel slammed against his skull. The shovel-head reverberated from the impact, sending vibrations through the handle.

The noise of metal impacting skull exploded into the night, echoing through the darkness.

Patrick Rose's face shut down, his screams ceased, as did the look of horror. He spun to the floor with a blank look of indifference, landing like a puppet on the muddy lawn. Lee dropped the shovel and breathlessly watched the injured maniac, whose barely conscious body continued to breathe—a wheezing whistle layered on each breath. Ahead of him, Zala was sitting on the ground with her knees pulled up to her chest. She gazed upon her beaten admirer and sobbed silently, tears of loss, relief, and fear dripping down reddened skin.

Rummaging through Patrick's pockets, Lee found the keys to the removal van. He gripped them tightly, paused to glance at Zala—she wasn't even looking his way, her eyes fixed on the black middle distance. He ran, skipping through the darkness as fast as he could. He could only see a few feet in front of him but he continued on at full pace, using his memory as a guide as his feet crossed over the muddy lawn and hopped onto the edge of the decking before dropping to the concrete path that ran down the side of the house.

He found the parked van. In his hand, he held a set of seven keys, all but one—a long thin and pointed key—looked exactly alike and he had no idea which one fit the lock.

With his entire body shaking from an intense adrenaline rush, he glanced from the van to his house, the keys trembling in his hand. He didn't know how to drive, but he did know how to use a phone.

Keeping the keys gripped tightly, the ribbed metal imprinting on his flesh, he bolted across the street. His breath spat out of his tired lungs in angry bursts. A welcome but short-lived sense of relief warmed him as he pushed his way into his house.

He tripped over the slumped body of the Lechnens' accomplice and flew through the air, crashing into the staircase. His right foot was the first to make contact, hitting one of the lower stairs moments before the rest of his body. It twisted in the crevice deep in the angle of the stair, and before he could pull it free or shift it away, the rest of his body crashed upon it.

His lungs screamed a mixture of obscenities and moans, his face an image of torture. With the entire weight of his body upon it, his ankle snapped like a twig, popping out of place before breaking in two.

He managed to bounce his body away from the stairs before his shins and knees suffered the same fate. Using his damaged ankle and outstretched arms, he sprung from the stairs just as quickly as he had fallen upon them. He rolled backward, past the stairs and over the dead man.

Screaming, he lifted his foot and observed the carnage. Looking at the devastation made the pain worse. His foot dangled off the end of his leg, every attempt to activate a nerve and move the appendage failed. It lulled from side to side like a slab of rubber.

A broken bone tried to force itself outward, a mound of skin protruded just above his ankle, but the bone hadn't penetrated. Gasping soft screams, he used the dead man in front of him to haul himself to his feet, immediately shifting his weight to his left foot.

The dangling foot dragged along the floor as he hopped to the living room, using the wall for support. He reached for the phone, almost diving on it when he spotted it. With fingers trembling at subsonic speeds, he tried to dial 999, hitting the correct sequence of numbers after six messy attempts.

"Police!" he screamed as soon as an operator answered. A heavy buzzing rang in his ears and the world around him spun madly.

Breathing heavily into the mouthpiece, he waited until he heard the operator. "There's a mad bastard trying to fucking kill me!" he screamed, pausing to swallow a large lump of dry saliva.

"Please calm down sir—"

The voice at the other end of the phone was nothing more than hazy static to his ears.

"I need help," he begged. "There are two people dead. Two more injured . . . maybe three." He felt a sickness rise up inside of him, he held it back. "He's a fucking psycho! He killed my wife, he killed his *own* wife, and now he's trying to kill me. Hurry up." He gave the operator his address and threw the phone across the room.

Skipping across the room, gritting his teeth to suppress the stabbing pain in his broken foot, he scooped up the set of car keys, which he had dropped on the stairs and then scuttled back into the night. He still didn't feel safe and he wanted to get as far away as possible.

25

When Lee reached the van, he threw his body against it. He had been walking on his floppy foot, pushing some of his weight onto it to keep a steady momentum in what was a desperate situation. He needed the van to take the weight off.

Fingering through the keys, he noticed his hands were still trembling madly, even worse than before. He had to use both of his hands just to make sure that the shaky extremities didn't carelessly drop the keys.

He struggled to fit the first key into the lock. His hands were shaking so much that they couldn't make the connection. He used both hands to steady it and drive it in.

The key squeezed in the lock but wouldn't turn.

He pulled it out angrily and searched for another one.

A scream from around the back of the Lechnen house forced him to stop. It was Zala. He turned instinctively to look at the house, thought for a few seconds, and then turned back to the door, breathlessly searching for another key.

Another key. Another failure. Another trembling moment of anger.

She screamed again, a muffled and helpless scream.

Lights popped on in the upstairs room of one of Lee's neighbors. Soon all the lights in the house flickered on, curtains were opened, and curious faces peered out.

Lee stopped what he was doing, staring blankly at the keys in his hand. His mind wandered. He took a long deep breath, shot one last look at the van door, closed his eyes, gritted his teeth, and ran.

Zala screamed again just as Lee's feet touched onto the paving slabs along the side of the house. His dangled foot dragged behind his leg like a ball and chain, twisting, turning, and roaming of its own accord.

In the middle of the garden, he saw the pair wrestling. Zala was trying to run away. Patrick, still on the ground, had grabbed one of her ankles with his uninjured hand and was trying to pull her down. She kicked at him aggressively and desperately, putting plenty of force into kicks that landed crushingly on Patrick's chest and stomach. One kick caught him square in the jaw, strong enough to splinter teeth, but he wasn't fazed. He continued to pull her down.

When Zala saw Lee hobbling across the garden, her eyes lit up. An overwhelming look of delight and relief spread across her face when he emerged from the darkness, red faced, sweating and determined.

He rushed over to her and grabbed her arm, trying to help her out of the quicksand that was Patrick Rose.

"She's mine!" Patrick spat. Blood sprayed out of his mouth as he spoke.

"Get off her," Lee demanded. He wanted to kick the mad man but knew he would either lose a foot or fall over.

"She's mine!" he called again.

Lee pulled away from Zala and removed his hands from her arm, taking a step back. She looked at him with desperate, pleading eyes. She needed his help and didn't want him to leave.

Lee had no intention of leaving. He fingered through the set of keys, picked out the long, thin one, and positioned it in the center of his palm, the rest of the keys pushed around the back of his hand, out of the way. He grabbed Patrick's hand, steadied his aim, and brought the pointed key down hard.

The key sunk into the flesh between Patrick's thumb and forefinger, cutting through his skin like warm butter. He quickly withdrew his grip, screaming like a cat caught in a bear-trap. He pulled his hand underneath his chest.

Zala immediately threw herself at Lee, stumbling into him. "Thanks," she said breathlessly.

Lee nearly fell backward. The extra weight caused a rush of pain which ran through his body like a bullet. Zala instantly recoiled, noticing his reaction. She looked down at his foot and cringed. "Are you okay?" she asked.

"Just fucking dandy," Lee spat through gritted teeth. He reached out and took her hand. "Come on."

Patrick tried to grab them, throwing a line of blood and an assault of obscenities as he swung his bloodied appendage their way. They ignored him and set off down the garden with Zala doing her best to support Lee's weight, leaving the moaning murderer wriggling on the grass.

They could hear action in the street. Nosy neighbors, curious watchers, poked their heads out through curtains and stood in doorways.

When they reached the van, Lee tossed Zala the keys. "You take them," he instructed as she caught them in her cupped hands, a startled, worried expression on her face.

He stood against the passenger door, agitated. His eyes flicked from the side of the Lechnen house to the windows in all the other houses in the street. He had a dozen eyes on him, some of them hiding behind curtains or doors, others staring. He cursed at them under his breath, eyeing them each in turn, none of them able to see his snarled expression.

"Hurry up," he called to Zala.

She fumbled just as messily as he had done. She dropped the keys, stared at them as they hit the floor, cursed her clumsiness and then, shaking and with tears in her eyes, she bent to pick them up before nearly dropping them again.

"Got it!" she shouted eventually, her words catching in her throat as relief kicked away a morsel of dread. She jammed the key in the lock and popped open the locks.

She jumped in first, watching through the window as Lee struggled with his own door. He saw her agitation, saw her eyes move from him to the darkened house, to the ignition, and then back again. He yanked open the door, threw himself inside, and glared at her.

She turned away, almost apologetic. Ashamed.

Lee didn't know where they were going, and he didn't care. He just wanted to get away. The police would sort out the mess he had created, but until then, the danger still remained.

Zala turned to him again. "Open the glove compartment," she instructed. Her breathing was rapid, worried. A strained string of moisture hung from her top lip to her bottom, stretching when she opened her mouth like the stitched-lip smile of a puppet. "There should be a gun inside."

Lee lingered on her lips, on her face, then turned away bitterly. He popped open the small compartment and looked inside. Buried amongst scrunched-up betting slips, notes, and sweet wrappers was a silver six-shooter, small enough to fit in the palm of his hand.

"You carry a gun?" he asked, incredulous. A part of him still remembered the Zala who wasn't out to get him; the Zala who hadn't nearly gotten him killed; the Zala who didn't just want his money and actually cared for his companionship.

"It's not mine," she said, managing to steady her shaking hands long enough to slide the key into the ignition. "It's Barry's," she explained. "The guy he shot."

The casual thief, the accidental killer, the indifferent victim. He had a name. Lee looked distrustfully at her but didn't say anything. Now wasn't the time.

She turned the key. The engine spluttered and spat momentarily before dying with a whimper. She tried again but it continued to wheeze like a dying smoker. "Fuck!" she screamed, smashing the steering wheel with her balled-up fists.

"Calm down," Lee said softly, despising the need he felt to reassure her. "We have time."

Zala turned to him, a flare of anger behind her eyes. "We don't have—" she paused, her words strangled, her mouth open. She remained in that eerie stance, staring blankly at Lee, until a small trickle of blood dripped out of her dried lips. Her body convulsed, coughed, and spat a torrent of crimson, coating the interior of the car. She fell forward, resting on Lee's lap.

He looked down to see a bullet wound in the back of her head, from which gushed a geyser of blood. He could feel her blood soaking into his crotch. Only then did he understand why his ears rang, and why his world had momentarily shaken.

He turned frantically toward the driver's side window. The glass had been penetrated with a clean, circular hole, ringed by spider-web fractures. Through the hole, standing a few feet away on the driveway, stood Patrick Rose, a gun held loosely in his shaking and bleeding hand. The play had reached its final act, and as Lee waited for the curtain to fall, shocked neighbors fumbled for their phones, refusing to avert their eyes or to leave the safety of their homes.

26

Lee could only watch in horror as Patrick slowly staggered up to the car. He thought about pushing Zala's body away, climbing out of the car and retreating to his house, but none of those tasks were easy or credible with a broken foot and a man following you with a gun.

Reaching the driver's side window, Rose allowed himself to fall against the van, using it as a support. The vehicle rocked ominously under his weight. He grunted roughly, muttering a soft and disbelieving laugh through pain-raked gums. He smiled through the glass at Lee, waving to him cheekily with his gun. He motioned for him to roll the window down and then pointed the pistol through the hole in the glass, reminding him of his intentions should he refuse.

Lee stared at the barrel for a moment, struggling to find a way out. Every inch of his body was screaming at him to run, but he would be shot down before he even clambered out of the car.

He gently lifted Zala's bleeding corpse from his lap. Her blood had soaked through his pants and was sticking to his thighs and groin. He didn't feel any remorse as he shoved her away; he had already mourned over the loss of the Zala he thought he knew.

"Where do you think you're going?" Patrick wondered placidly, peering into the car like a police officer about to hand over a ticket.

He stuck his face inside the van and ran his eyes over the slumped female form. "Such a waste," he said, shaking his head. "Just like Jennifer. But . . . " He brightened up, "That's women for you. They get what they deserve in the end. Isn't that right, Lee?"

"I wouldn't know."

"She was trying to con you. She wanted to use your good nature against you to rob you blind. Don't you think she deserved to die?"

Lee looked indifferently at Zala, her body propped up on the driver's side, her eyes staring coldly into the roof of the car. Her blood was turning the beige interior into a sickly burgundy.

"I'm not one to judge."

She didn't deserve to die. No matter how much she had hurt him, how much she had *tried* to hurt him, he didn't think she deserved death. She was misguided, cold, unsympathetic perhaps, but they weren't traits that warranted death. He knew that, yet he didn't feel the slightest pity for her now that her body was growing cold and her blood was drying on his pants.

"What comes around goes around, right? She tried to fuck you over and in the end she lost her husband and then her life. That's what they call karma, right?"

"That's not karma. That's just an evil dickhead with a gun."

Patrick laughed softly, unperturbed by the insult. "Don't you believe that everyone eventually gets what they deserve?"

Lee looked sternly at Rose. They stared at each other momentarily before Lee replied with a slow, meaningful nod—a warning that went unnoticed.

Patrick smiled. "And she certainly got what was coming to her. As did Jennifer—"

"Jennifer was a fucking saint," Lee snapped. "I don't care what you and her got up to. I don't care what she did. She was a good person."

"She committed adultery and murder," Patrick pushed.

"What about you?" Lee wanted to know. "How many people have *you* killed? How many lives have you destroyed? If there is such a cosmic force as karma, then believe me, you have a whole world of pain heading your way."

"Maybe, maybe not. Every rule has an exception, after all."

Lee was lost for words, unable to understand the smiling sociopath. "Fuck you," he said softly and without conviction.

"Get out of the car," Patrick ordered, waving the gun.

Lee gently pushed the door open and slowly climbed out. He noticed the street had gone quiet again. Those watching the slaughter had now retired to the safety of their houses, hiding behind thick, suburban walls and callous ignorance. No doubt the police had received more worried calls though. Soon the area would be flooded with panda cars and riot vans.

"How can you still think of Jennifer as a saint?" Patrick wanted to know as he motioned for Lee to join him on the other side of the vehicle. "She cheated on you. She lied to you. She was telling you how much she loved you, kissing you good-bye, and then coming across the road to fuck me. She didn't care for your feelings and didn't even think twice about my wife's feelings. Saints show compassion, she showed none. Don't you think she deserved to die?"

Lee, whose chin had been resting on his chest, raised his eyes to stare directly into the eyes of the maniac. "I loved her," he said with commitment. "She didn't deserve to die and neither did Zala. What the fuck is wrong with you?"

"What's wrong with *me*? Let me see . . . you cut my hand open with a key and busted the other one with a shovel *and* you clouted me around the head."

Lee couldn't help but smile. "You had it coming."

Patrick's face quickly flashed with anger and he lashed out. He drove his head forward, bouncing his forehead off Lee's in a high-impact head-butt that sent Lee sprawling.

Lee fell backward, holding his left hand against his head and keeping his right by his side. He bounced off the side of the van and sprang back upright again. He used the momentum to his advantage and jumped forward, flying at Patrick. Tired body slammed into tired body as both men wrestled to the ground.

Patrick's gun flew from his grasp under the strain of the impact. It slid down the driveway, screeching against the concrete before slamming into the garage door with a metallic shudder.

Fists, knees, and elbows collided as they each tried to gain an advantage. Patrick tried to use his teeth, snapping like a tormented alligator. He ate mouthfuls of clothing before he eventually gnawed on skin, taking a small chunk of flesh from Lee's upper arm.

The bite was barely felt and Lee responded by driving his knee into Patrick's groin. The psychopath squealed like a pig, then, freeing his hands, he grabbed Lee by the throat and squeezed.

Lee flipped over and the two men continued to roll, moving away from the van. Turning over on the cold tarmac and the wet grass, fists pounded flesh, fingernails grasped at skin, eyes, and orifices. Knees and feet clawed at bone.

A muffled blast of gunfire erupted between the two bodies, followed by a blood-curdling scream that spat out in shock and horror. After the deathly howl, the rolling stopped. The fight was over.

They rolled away from each other and struggled to get to their feet. Lee was the first to rise. He stood with the aid of his rubber foot, applying weight to it with little care, apathetic to the pain.

In his hand, he held the small silver gun taken from the van's glove compartment. A six-shooter now with five bullets in the chamber. He pointed the smoking barrel at the wriggling killer.

"*You fuck!*" Patrick shouted, his voice strained through a sheet of agony. "I'm going to fucking rip you apart." His hands gripped his stomach, holding back the blood that gushed from a wound above his naval.

Lee stood over him, aiming the gun down. "Feel free to try."

Patrick looked up at the weapon, staring directly into the barrel before moving his gaze to Lee's face. He released a stuttering, painful laugh.

"Is something funny?" Lee wondered.

"This is a turn out for the books, isn't it?" Patrick aimed the laughter at himself. "*This* certainly wasn't part of the plan."

"You ruined my life," Lee accused. "You killed the only person I ever loved, the only person to ever love—" he stopped and let the rest of his words fade away. He wasn't sure of their validity anymore.

Patrick laughed harder, at Lee this time. "You sad, sad bastard!" he spat. "The only girl you ever loved and she didn't give a *shit* about you. She was probably the only one to actually like you and well . . . " He laughed mockingly. "She didn't. You might as well turn that gun on yourself, you have nobody." Still gripping his stomach, he lifted his head off the ground with great effort and spat at Lee. "You have *nothing.*"

Lee casually stared at the glob of saliva that landed on his knee, soaking into his trousers below the crimson stain. "You're wrong," he said, bringing his attention back to Patrick. "I have money. I have a house. Jennifer gave you cheap thrills and a ticket to whatever fucked-up state you're in now, but she gave me a fortune. She gave me a chance."

"The money would have been mine," Patrick spat. "We were going to live together. We were going to *be* together." His words lacked venom.

"You still can," Lee said simply.

"What?"

He grinned broadly. "Give her a kiss from me." He waited just long enough for Patrick's face to change to horrified realization, then he pulled the trigger.

Patrick's scream was delayed. He thought the bullet was heading for his face. He thought the gunshot would be the last sound he heard. The bullet struck lower then he had anticipated though. It crushed and splintered his right knee cap, tearing it away and nearly separating his lower leg.

"What the fuck!" His words cracked in his throat.

Lee laughed, a light of sadism in his eyes.

"Maybe you're right about this karma thing," he pondered aloud.

Patrick lifted his head to look at his knee and then dropped it back to the floor, wishing he hadn't. The extreme pain caused his muscles to twitch uncontrollably as blood gushed from various wounds. Turning his head to the side, he coughed and sputtered, saliva dripping from his mouth like clear glue, before vomiting violently on the concrete.

The sick was minimal, barely enough to fill a cup, but his nausea was intense.

"Nasty," Lee said with a grin.

Patrick continued to wretch. Some of the vomit splashed onto his face, some dripped from his bottom lip. "You bastard," he shouted up at Lee, his words barely audible.

He tried to sit up, the vomit catching in his throat. He shifted his weight to his uninjured leg and used his hands to push himself upward. The process was long and painful for him and, as soon as he managed to sit, Lee kicked him back to the floor again.

"What the fuck are you doing?" Patrick demanded to know.

"Call it karma." He raised the gun and aimed it at Patrick's other leg. The bullet shattered shinbone and penetrated to the ground beneath.

Patrick's screams rang out into the night, sending fear into the hearts and minds of anyone who heard them.

"Zala, Riso, and Jennifer couldn't let things sort themselves out. What goes around comes around, but for them, what came around was you," Lee explained. "People don't always get what's coming to them, at least not to the extent they deserve."

"What do you want?"

The neighbors were watching. All eyes in the street blinked through the darkness to catch sight of the mad dance beneath the streetlights. They were getting their fill. They were witnessing their killer as he prepared to kill.

"I want to make sure you suffer as much as possible," Lee explained. "I have three bullets left and probably about ten minutes before the police get here. That gives me three minutes per bullet and then one to finish you off before anyone can save you." He paused and grinned, beaming sadistically into the glassy eyes of the man who had killed his wife. "So tell me, Patrick. Where would you like to be shot next?" He aimed the gun at Rose's groin while he waited for the screaming man to decide.

EPILOGUE

A year later

The young couple loved what they saw, and they saw everything. Here a nursery; perfect for little Jimmy or Julie, now just a glint in their eye but soon, fingers crossed, a double-line on a pregnancy test. There a game room, for him of course, he was the gamer, the pool player, the darts enthusiast, but she liked to dabble. Here a spare room, for when their parents came over to visit. There a second spare room, for when *he* pissed *her* off and she decided the spare room was too good for him.

There were possibilities for a conservatory; a place to while away their summer nights and their spring holidays, to get drunk and watch the sun go down, to party and revel in their friendships; and an aviary, home to their two squawking parrots, which cost a small fortune and were doted-on hand and foot.

It was perfect.

"I still don't understand why you're selling this place," he declared as he stood outside the house, fondly looking at the large facade, his wife tucked comfortably in the crook of his loving arm. "And for so cheap."

Joseph Lee reciprocated their friendly smiles and then turned back to his house, his home for many years. He gave them a casual shrug. "It's complicated. Let's just say I need a new start."

"What about the neighbors?" he asked, deciding to change the subject in case the homeowner changed his mind. "Are they okay?"

Lee instinctively glanced over the road. The menacing structure of house 23 glared back.

"Does anyone live there?" the man asked, following Lee's gaze.

Lee calmly shook his head, a somber chill invading him. "Not for a while. The owners were a—" he paused, looked at them each in turn, smiled as broadly as he could. "A little crazy. They're not around anymore. Solicitors are still going over the estate, you know how it is."

"Ah," the man said with a nod. "Bureaucracy."

"Something like that."

"And the rest of the neighbors?"

Lee glanced up and down the street. Curtains flickered, curious heads were already on the lookout. He caught the gaze of the next-door neighbor, an elderly woman, and she ducked back into her house, out of sight.

The same woman had pestered him at every opportunity she had over the last year. After the incident in the street, over which Lee had been cleared—his vengeance ruled as self-defense, the whole mess judged to be the work of others—the little old lady had bugged him and annoyed him at every opportunity. She insisted he was a serial killer, even tried to get him evicted from his own home via a number of bizarre applications to a powerless council.

He didn't mind. He was leaving now, but it had nothing to do with her. If anything, he wanted to stay just to annoy her, and others like her, of which there were many.

"They're okay," Lee lied. "You'll have a good life here, I can see it."

The man and the woman exchanged smiles, shook Lee's hand, and then bid him good-bye. The house would be theirs in a little over two weeks.

When the new homeowners had departed and the curious, beady eyes of the neighbors tired of the actionless scene in front of the Lee household, Joseph looked at his house for the last time. He wouldn't be staying there tonight, or at all. He'd already moved out, his belongings—everything of value, and nothing of Jennifer's—were already in his new house. A house miles away from the backward town that had annoyed, angered, and accused him for two years.

His thoughts were interrupted by a sharp report from a car horn. He turned around to see a car pull to a stop behind him. Its occupant, a young woman wearing sunglasses to shade the glaring afternoon sun—her long golden hair draping over her sun-beaten face—climbed out of the car and offered Joseph a warm smile.

"Saying your good-byes?" she said.

He grinned and walked up to her. They kissed, hugged. He stood back, his hands on her shoulders, his eyes gazing into hers.

He had met Emma not long after the ordeal. She was a nurse and had helped to patch him together after Patrick Rose and the Lechnens' had beaten and broken him. They became close, and he had told her everything. She became as infatuated with him as he was with her.

She wasn't rich, wasn't high-class, and wasn't elegant. She was young, pretty. A little pudgy around the waist but beautiful for it. She was sometimes shy, rarely outgoing, but often introspective, thoughtful, and meek. She wasn't what he would have thought of as his type, yet from the moment he first saw her, first heard her speak, first received her tender and healing touch, he knew she was perfect for him. She was everything he needed and wanted, and, most importantly, she looked nothing like Jennifer. Or Zala.

"Let's go home," he said softly.